Anupam Shrivastava, a telecommunications engineer by profession, has over three decades of experience working in the public-sector telecommunications industry, including the Department of Telecommunications, Telecommunications Consultants India Ltd, and Bharat Sanchar Nigam Ltd. He was posted in Bhopal, his hometown, when the Babri Masjid was demolished in December 1992, and witnessed the immediate fallout of that event on the city and its people. He retired in 2019 as the Chairman and Managing Director of Bharat Sanchar Nigam Ltd. He lives in Delhi and Bhopal. This is his first novel.

BHOPAL '92

A Novel

ANUPAM SHRIVASTAVA

SPEAKING TIGER

In association with VYAKTI

SPEAKING TIGER BOOKS LLP
125A, Ground Floor, Shahpur Jat, near Asiad Village,
New Delhi 110049

First published by Speaking Tiger Books in 2024

ISBN: 978-93-5447-812-3
eISBN: 978-93-5447-752-2

10 9 8 7 6 5 4 3 2 1

Typeset in Sabon LT Std by SÜRYA, New Delhi
Printed at HT Media Ltd, Greater Noida

To Aria,
my granddaughter.

CONTENTS

Author's Note

'Who will read your book, Papa?' My son's inquiry, delivered without him lifting his gaze from the laptop screen displaying the manuscript of this book, struck me as profoundly significant. His direct question prodded me to realise that holding this book in your hands does not imply that you have an inherent reason to read it.

In writing this preface, I hope to provide an answer to my son's question and a glimpse into the journey that lies ahead for those who choose to embark on this literary adventure.

This true story, dramatised in terms of the plot and events, and peppered with creative liberties to engage readers, revolves around four transformative days that echo the adage, '*Zindagi char din ki hoti hai.*' (Life is but four short days.)

In this tale spanning four days, I try to unearth life's essence. While writing it, I discovered boundless human potential and the nuanced nature of the truth, which is akin to the layers of an onion. The fleeting moments in this book encapsulate a lifetime, a journey of self-discovery.

I worked as a telecom engineer in the government sector for more than three decades, holding leadership positions from the district level to the national level, and retired as the Chairman and Managing Director of Bharat Sanchar Nigam Limited.

This book is about how I kept the telecommunication network running during religious violence and rioting, in which hundreds of people were killed, in an otherwise peaceful Bhopal. This was in the aftermath of the demolition of the Babri Masjid in Ayodhya on December 6, 1992—an event that shook up and redefined the polity of our nation.

Communication in its modern avatar—our mobile phone and internet network—is shut down in case of a clash, communal or otherwise, a law and order problem, or even in anticipation of such events. This is done to prevent people from connecting and, through that process, galvanising support against the government. It is also done to curtail the spread of rumours that instigate people against the government or each other. This has become a standard operating procedure, as some recent events suggest. Of course, the government machinery has its own parallel communications network, which continues to function unhindered.

Way back in the 1990s, before the information revolution reached the Indian subcontinent, the situation was very different. To be able to communicate via a phone was a luxury. Only a select few had telephones, and long-distance calling was expensive. There used to be a waiting list of years, and the cost of breaking the queue was no less than a year's salary for a 'Group A' government officer. Besides, communications were kept running manually, and the task was fairly industrious in nature.

In those days, for the first time, we read George Orwell's chillingly prophetic novel *1984*, exploring a future where communications would become a tool of government control. As communication engineers, we also envisioned ourselves as proud architects of a new order that would tremendously empower India. Within the society, our role commanded respect, surpassing even that of uniformed officials, and sometimes, we were feared more than the top Income Tax Department bureaucrats! Police officials took pride in knowing a trunk operator, who was indispensable for making swift connections.

Today, society celebrates pocket-sized communication gadgets, but back then, pride lay in knowing an official of the telephone department. This novel explores that transformative era when being able to communicate over the phone was still a luxury.

In that day and age, the city of Bhopal had come to a grinding halt after the Babri Masjid's demolition. A curfew was imposed, people were forced to stay home, and yet many people hit the streets to orchestrate clashes, resulting in mayhem and bloodshed. People spread rumours via loudspeakers mounted on vehicles, creating fear and uncertainty and provoking mistrust and hatred between the two numerically biggest communities in the country and the city.

Most employees who ran the telephone exchange couldn't come to work, so I stayed at work for four days with a handful of staff to keep the telecommunication networks running. It was of critical importance to be connected at a time when the law-and-order machinery had collapsed, and outside help was required to deal with an unprecedented crisis.

But despite the fear and uncertainty, we did it.

Those arduous but adventurous days fill me with a sense of achievement even today. We did our work, despite unrest and bloodshed weighing us down mentally and emotionally.

Since the advent of the internet age, each person has become the creator and disseminator of information, and tools exist that can make the unreal look real. The changed perspectives on telecom and communications have changed the responses to these innovations.

In my long career, I have also witnessed State-owned enterprises being unfairly disparaged, and I hope this book will help set the record straight. I have heard Bharat Sanchar Nigam Ltd being belittled as 'Bhai Sahab Nahi Lagta'. Although BSNL was set up in 2002, after the events described in this book, it is still my ardent hope to convey the dedication of the employees of public enterprises, particularly in the telecoms industry, the sacrifices it takes to run a communication service in a challenging, dangerous time, and the progression of technology in the sector, which would not have happened if State-owned enterprises did not herald change, not to mention, foot the bill!

In all these ways, this book is also a people's history of how communication changes the way we live and die.

Anupam Shrivastava
April 23, 2024

तू हिन्दु बनेगा ना मुसलमान बनेगा
इन्सान की औलाद है इन्सान बनेगा
तू हिन्दु बनेगा ना मुसलमान बनेगा
इन्सान की औलाद है इन्सान बनेगा

You shall not become Hindu or Muslim
For you are born of humankind
You shall become a human
Transcending the divisions that bind.

CHAPTER ONE

Wrong Place at the Wrong Time

December 7, 1992

It was Monday morning, and, as always, my day began early. At around 7 a.m., I pulled the curtains from one of the windows of my ancestral home in anticipation of any light that the winter sun could muster. However, I was greeted by a thick December fog, covering all of Bhopal with near-zero visibility.

Within an hour, I donned my neatly ironed khaki Safari suit: an untucked, long, square-cut jacket worn with trousers. Wearing a Safari suit didn't prepare bureaucrats like me for an expedition. Instead, these suits were the default attire of government servants and the hallmark of the Indian bureaucracy during the 1990s.

At 9 a.m., a blue Mahindra Jeep—my unofficial official ride—announced its arrival at the main gate of my house with a crisp honk. The E-3 Sector of the

Arera Colony where I lived was the poshest residential locality in Bhopal. As I walked out of my drawing room and entered the porch, where my driver, young Mustafa Khan, was there to pick me up, I glanced at my wife, Tripti, and our two little boys, Mohit and Ankit, aged three and five. I said my goodbyes to them and stepped out to face the day.

Soon, we were en route to the Arera Telephone Exchange—my workplace—in the blue jeep with 'Government of India' painted in bold red just above its windscreen. In a sense, this jeep was the SUV of yesteryears, but unlike the cosy interiors of the SUVs we have today, it offered little comfort. Typical to the style of government vehicles in those days, the jeep had sturdy but cushioned seats, and they were draped with clean, ivory-white towels.

I sat in the long front seat as the jeep rolled out of the house and picked up speed, a chill wind brushing past my face. I did not realise it then, but soon, I would be playing a crucial role in the larger scheme of things set to unfold in Bhopal from that day on.

Here I was, a central government official working in a State-owned telecom company in the capital of Madhya Pradesh, in charge of ensuring that the communication lines in the city always remained functional. This task would have been mundane and devoid of gut-wrenching challenges on any other day but that day.

However, the events of the day before, December

6, 1992, would leave their imprint not merely on the annals of modern Indian history but on the collective psyche of the entire nation. About 800 kilometres Northeast of Bhopal, in Ayodhya town in neighbouring Uttar Pradesh, activists commonly known as kar sevaks, belonging to a Hindu group, had demolished a mosque built in the 16th century.

The kar sevaks believed that the mosque had been named after the first Mughal emperor, Zahir-ud-Din Muhammad Babar. They also said that the mosque had been built on Babar's imperial orders and that the site it stood on was the birthplace of Lord Rama.

Many residents of Ayodhya and a significant section of the Hindu population across India believed that the mosque had been built by destroying an ancient temple dedicated to the Hindu God, Rama.

The Babri Masjid was a disputed structure. However, that had been no mere legal dispute between the followers of two of India's numerically largest faiths. It had enormous potential to incite crowds, and, on that day after the demolition, almost every nook and cranny of the country was in a state of undeclared emergency.

I had learned of the demolition from the news the previous day, but I experienced its impact on Bhopal first-hand only on my drive to work. As my house receded in the rearview mirror, I sensed a peculiar stillness pervading that day. Mustafa and I rode in awkward silence on the familiar streets.

Truth be told, I had not been able to pinpoint what exactly had conjured up the disquieting silence in the city. After all, I rationalised, Ayodhya was hundreds of miles away from Bhopal. Even the traffic in the city was moving at its usual pace, and someone new to Bhopal might even have thought that it was business as usual in the market areas. But with their deserted look, the lanes and by-lanes that I knew so well told me a different story.

Perhaps Mustafa felt my discomfort because just then, he pushed a cassette into the jeep's music player, and an old Hindi song instantly played, lifting our mood with its soul-stirring lyrics:

तू हिन्दु बनेगा ना मुसलमान बनेगा
इन्सान की औलाद है इन्सान बनेगा
तू हिन्दु बनेगा ना मुसलमान बनेगा
इन्सान की औलाद है इन्सान बनेगा

(You shall not become Hindu or Muslim
For you are born of humankind
You shall become a human
Transcending the divisions that bind.)

That was the exact moment when I told myself that the demolition of the mosque would be of little significance to us in Bhopal, which had a long history of communitarian harmony. The Chief Minister of Madhya Pradesh, Sunder Lal Patwa, fondly known as Patwa-ji, had already assured that everybody would be safe and that there was no reason to panic. So, though

I understood why this event could polarise the popular imagination, little did I know of the extent to which it would change the political narrative of the nation, nor that thousands of innocent lives would meet a horrible end in its wake.

~

Mustafa had joined as my driver on a casual basis quite recently. He had been recommended for the job by his elder brother, Nawab Khan, a union leader of drivers in Bhopal. Mustafa was charismatic and handsome and spoke Hindi with a thick Bhopali accent. Almost a decade later, when I saw Bollywood actor Shahid Kapoor's debut film, I realised that Mustafa bore a striking resemblance to him.

But as we continued towards my office, the song made the mood in the jeep seemingly conflict with the eerie noiselessness and uncertainty in my hometown. It is Mustafa who spoke up first. 'Sir,' he began, '*Main ke riya tha, aaj thoda alag mahaul ban riya hai. Humari colony mein kal raat se naarey lag riye hain.*' Mustafa was right, the air was thick with fear. I had heard about the slogan-shouting on the local TV news channels. Mustafa was confirming that he himself had witnessed it all.

When I asked him what kinds of slogans he had heard, Mustafa turned to look at me and corroborated more of the news reports. '*Kya batayen, Sir, log patakhey chhuda riye they aur chillaa riye they ki mandir wahin banayenge*,' he said, adding, '*Aur hamarey log bhi ke riye they, "Hum majjid todney ka badla lengey, danga phaila dengey*."'

'*Hamarey log*?' I echoed Mustafa's reference to 'his people', though I had guessed his meaning. He meant that while the Hindus were celebrating the demolition of the Babri Masjid by setting off firecrackers and proclaiming that they would build a temple where the mosque had stood, members of his community, the Muslims, were angrily proclaiming that as vengeance for the demolition, they would spark violence.

'*Arey, kya Sir*,' he scoffed at me in response. '*Hamarey miyan bhai*,' he said, dropping his voice when he said 'Muslim brethren'.

I looked at him with concern and, changing the conversation topic, wondered aloud why he had come in to work amid the disturbances in his locality.

'*Arey nahi, Sir. Aap kay liye to jaan haazir hai, kya? Koi aapko kuchh boley, toh pehley main samney aaunga, kya*?' he responded. I was touched. Mustafa had just offered to lay down his life to protect me. All I had to do was ask, he had said, and he would stand between me and any attacker. He was getting a little emotional.

The 'kya' he appended to some of his sentences literally meant 'what' but conveyed a meaning akin to 'you know' in English. It is a part of the conversational style in the Bhopali dialect. It usually gets the listener to nod or smile in affirmation.

Since I had no direct experience of the situation in his neighbourhood or elsewhere in Bhopal, I, too, smiled in response, partly because Mustafa's eccentric declarations of loyalty moved me and partly because of his Bhopali dialect.

Then I told him not to worry, and repeated the latest statement of the Chief Minister for his benefit. 'Hasn't Patwa-ji announced on the radio that Bhopal never witnessed sectarian violence? He has said nobody would be allowed to tarnish its harmony,' I reminded him.

'Haan, Sir,' he replied, nodding in agreement, and began to regale me with stories about his father and grandfather, who had also lived in Bhopal. He said his late father would describe Indian civilisation as a grand fusion of its two religious streams, like the confluence of the Ganga and Jamuna, the two great rivers of its Northern plains. He also narrated his great-grandfather's decision to shelter Hindu migrants from Pakistan during India's Partition.

Even in those tumultuous months when the country was being split in two, there had been no riots in Bhopal, Mustafa claimed. He took evident pride in his personal history and Bhopal's famed religious tolerance.

I complimented his forefathers and then patted him on the shoulder. Mustafa's chest seemed to swell with pride. For the rest of the journey, he explained to me how his family's fortunes had dwindled after his father's generation, mostly because of the lack of education in the Muslim community, especially in his generation.

At least the song playing on the stereo had now synchronised with the subject of our conversation, if not the events outside. The music had lasted for the duration of our commute. As we arrived near the main gate of the Arera Telephone Exchange, the last stanza was about to conclude its musical symphony.

नफ़रत जो सिखाये वो धरम तेरा नहीं है
इन्सां को जो रौंदे वो कदम तेरा नहीं है
कुरआन न हो जिसमे वो मंदिर नहीं तेरा
गीता न हो जिसमे वो हरम तेरा नहीं है

(The religion that teaches hatred is not yours
No step that tramples humans is yours
No temple is yours where there is no Quran
The Kaaba is not yours if it has no Gita.)

The Arera Telephone Exchange was adjacent to the Madhya Pradesh Legislative Assembly, which meant that my office was supposedly in one of the safest parts of the state, immune to any threats of violence.

As a Divisional Engineer (Internal) in the Government of India's Department of Telecommunication—popularly known as the Door Sanchar Vibhag or Telephone Department—it was my responsibility to oversee the telephone exchanges in Bhopal. The city had two primary exchanges, the City Exchange and the Arera Exchange, which we were driving to. My work required me to juggle between these two exchanges almost every day.

Usually, Mustafa ferried me to the Arera Exchange in the first half of the day and then he drove me to the City Exchange in the second half. But that day, just before we reached the Arera Exchange, I decided to change the routine and go to the City Exchange first. The sudden change in plans meant that Mustafa had to turn the jeep around and reach our destination via Sultania Road in the Jahangirabad locality and past Pul Pukhta. It was not the usual route we took to get there from the Arera Exchange. And so, though we didn't know it then, we were now destined to drive through a locality where rioting had indeed erupted after the events of December 6, ostensibly for the first time in Bhopal's history.

When our jeep reached Jahangirabad Square, and we were about to turn left towards Pul Pukhta, we spotted a raucous mob running in our general direction from the right side of another crossing on the Chiklod Road. They waved sticks, brandished swords, and carried burning torches. We saw the skull caps worn by the restless assemblage. Young men in their twenties, and even some fifteen-or-sixteen-year-olds, were racing around, raising slogans: 'Allah-hu-Akbar' and 'maaro', 'kaato', 'nestnaboot kardo'. ('God is great!' 'kill them', 'cut them to pieces', 'destroy them'.)

Public safety seemed to have become an obsolete idea, and mob rule prevailed. We saw columns of smoke rising in the background, framed by the silhouette of the gang approaching us. It meant that shops and properties had been set on fire by this mob or another just like it.

Worse, the rioters were chasing a heavily outnumbered police force. Watching the policemen run helter-skelter for their lives was a demoralising sight. Many officers had torn uniforms visibly stained with blood.

The adrenaline rush had numbed my mind for a second or two, but now, I heard my racing heart. Here I was, a central government officer with no security, stuck at the wrong place at the wrong time.

Once again, Mustafa broke the silence.

'*Yeh log kya kar riye hain? Kaunsi dushmani ho gayi hai? Police itni majboor kyun hai?*' (What are people doing? Why so much enmity? Why are the police so helpless?) he said in complete bewilderment.

His arms trembled on the steering wheel.

I could only say, '*Kuch pata nahi.*' It was my failed attempt to hide the fear growing within me, for I truly did not know what to do next. I saw no way out of our situation.

Mustafa slammed hard on the brakes, and we came to a screeching halt. The sound of the jeep drew the mob's attention towards us, and, seeing a government vehicle, it began to run straight towards us. Hundreds of pairs of eyes stared at the jeep with hatred, anger, and a discernible eagerness to destroy everything in their path, including us.

I knew the dangers of mob mentality, herd

psychology, and crowd behaviour in general, but experiencing it was something my rational mind was unprepared for.

I knew the mob had collectively read 'Government of India' emblazoned on the jeep's front side. Those words had always evoked pride in me, but that day, they made me and my driver prime targets.

The rioters seemed to have lost interest in the retreating policemen and shouted slogans around us. I imagined all that they could do to us. Their brightly burning torches made me imagine the possibility of getting immolated along with the jeep.

Despite the chilly December morning, beads of sweat trickled down Mustafa's forehead, and his breathing was shallow and rapid. His mouth hung open in apprehension.

The fact that the mob shared its religion with Mustafa didn't matter to him. He looked at me to seek the next course of action. The reassurances he had made a few minutes back about sacrificing his life seemed forgotten.

I knew that I must push back my fears and act rationally if we were to survive the approaching mob.

Mustafa was about to engage the reverse gear of the jeep when I stopped him. The charging crowd would have easily caught up with our slow getaway in reverse. I asked him to accelerate instead, and then take the sharp left turn towards Pul Pukhta.

Instantly, as if under a spell, Mustafa revved the

engine and drove towards the crowd at the highest speed he could manage. The jeep brushed against some of the attackers, at which he shrieked incoherently. Then he looked in the rear-view mirror and saw the mob slowly disappearing. A sigh of relief escaped his lips.

Suddenly, there was a loud thud as someone sent a stone flying at us, which struck the rear of the jeep, but it was a small price for having been in the wrong place at this time. As we sped away, we saw reinforcements reach the police personnel whom the mob had been chasing. Just a minute had passed, but the police seemed to be planning its next move to tackle the enraged posse.

~

Finally, we were in the vicinity of our destination, the City Telephone Exchange. The sight of the building brought relief, but it was to be short-lived. About 100 metres from the main gate, we encountered a procession of saffron-clad Hindus, shouting slogans at the top of their voices.

Written all over their faces was a sense of triumph over the demolition of the disputed structure in Ayodhya. Their eyes sparkled with joy, and their lips curved into wide smiles. They filled the air with slogans about accomplishment and celebration. The intensity of their passion sent shivers down my spine, and I felt uneasy, even though they were unarmed.

The closer we got to the procession, the louder the cacophony grew. Its sloganeering consisted of '*Ram Lala Hum Aayenge, Mandir Wahin Banayenge*,' the high-profile slogan about building a temple dedicated to Lord Rama at the site of the demolished mosque, and 'Jai Shri Ram' and 'Har-Har Mahadev', in praise of Hindu gods.

This crowd was heterogeneous. Its members belonged to every age group and each socio-economic stratum. All the members of the procession seemed united for a singular cause. Their eyes were filled with such extraordinary devotion and commitment that I found it difficult to comprehend their intention.

The shopkeepers in the area had sensed trouble was looming. Mustafa and I watched them as they quickly lowered the shutters of their stores. It was my turn to experience what Mustafa had felt just minutes ago. This crowd was raising slogans championing the cause of the Hindus, but I couldn't find anything relatable to them. Instead, I felt scared about what this mindlessly passionate crowd was capable of doing.

As the crowd milled between the jeep and the entrance to the telephone exchange, I realised that it would be impossible to drive into the premises. So, I stepped out, asking Mustafa to wait at a distance and enter the exchange building once the road had cleared.

Miraculously, even after wading through two mobs and facing the immediate threat of violence, I had arrived at my office on time, at around 10 a.m. What I didn't know was that my experiences so far on December 7, 1992 would be eclipsed by what was about to unfold in the city over the next few days.

I instantly felt secure upon entering the exchange building. Overlooking the splashes of paan that had been spat into the corners of the corridors, which would have triggered my temper on normal days, I went straight to my office and slumped into the chair. I felt drained after the most traumatic commute of my bureaucratic career.

As I sat, visuals of the Babri Masjid being demolished flashed through my mind. By now, these sights had been seen by all Bhopalis on cable TV channels and were also published in the morning and evening newspapers. They would consume my thoughts for days, weeks, even years, and leave an indelible mark on my consciousness.

This demolition itself was preceded by a chain of events, which began after an idol of Lord Rama was discovered in the Babri complex in 1949. This discovery changed the very nature of the title dispute between the Hindu and Muslim parties over the ownership of the site.

Now, the consequences of the demolition were to follow. The capital of Madhya Pradesh was about to break from its harmonious past and witness its most horrifying violence in decades. The peaceful coexistence of adherents to the city's two prominent faiths would undergo a seismic shift, and the wounds of the rioting to follow would prove to be slow to heal.

My feeling of safety was disrupted by loud voices outside my office chamber. A heated argument was on. I rushed out of the room. It was Uttam Sharma, the leader of a workers' union in the telephone exchange, and Aziz Ahmad, a member of the same union.

Uttam Sharma was called Dada, which means 'elder brother', out of respect by his fellow union members. They stood facing each other in the long corridor of the exchange building, their voices rising with every passing moment. The animosity between them was palpable as they argued.

'It had to be done, Aziz! We have protected our religion and culture, which were in danger,' Uttam exclaimed, his face distorted by anger.

'But at what cost, Dada? Think of the destruction and the suffering it is already bringing. How can we justify violence in the name of religion?' Aziz responded, equally loud and passionate.

'You don't understand! The Babri Masjid stood on the spot where Lord Rama was born. We could not allow that insult to our faith and heritage,' Uttam scoffed at Aziz's words.

Aziz's face fell, and his voice broke. 'Dada, what about those who worshipped at the mosque? What about our feelings and our beliefs?' he asked.

Uttam took one step forward, eyes blazing with conviction. 'Our religion teaches us to defend our beliefs and gods, Aziz. The kar sevaks had no choice but to demolish the structure, which was never a mosque in the first place,' he said.

'How can you say this, Dada?' shouted Aziz, also taking a step forward.

'Not just me—many historians believe Babri Masjid only symbolised the homosexual equation of Babar and the slave boy-lover, Baburi,' Uttam responded angrily.

'And was demolishing it the only solution?' asked Aziz.

Then, the two men stood, staring at each other, speechless for a moment. Their silence was pregnant with suppressed thoughts and emotions. The sounds of their raised voices echoing down the corridor reminded me of the deep rift created by the demolition of the mosque in Ayodhya. I wondered how society would ever reconcile these growing differences—would it ever?

Uttam and Aziz began arguing again in voices full of hatred, forgetting how, just days ago, they had celebrated the victory of their union with red gulaal, the coloured powder used on the Holi festival and other celebrations, and garlands of flowers.

Seeing them argue made me realise that the hatred I believed had disappeared once I entered the telephone exchange had already infiltrated my workplace. I had to intervene to try and calm them down and defuse the situation. As I approached them, I could see despair in their eyes.

'Uttam Sharma, Aziz Ahmad, what is going on here?' I asked in a firm but gentle voice.

They turned to me with shocked expressions as if I had caught them red-handed. I felt some ease, as their dismay indicated that they knew their behaviour was out of line. Both inhaled deep breaths as if preparing to resume their argument, but then they realised where they were and that a senior official was standing before them.

'Dada believes that the demolition of the Babri Masjid was necessary, while I think it was a terrible tragedy that can divide people and take lives,' Aziz complained, trembling with passion.

I felt the weight of their conflicting views, the sadness and anger dominating their otherwise reasonable minds. But I knew that arguing and fighting were useless.

'Look, this is a complicated and emotional topic. But we need to find a way to move forward and work for a better future for everybody,' I said, trying to extinguish the tension.

They seemed to agree, for I noticed relief flash across their faces. All they needed was someone to hear them out and try to sort out their differences, I thought. Maybe there was a larger lesson for society in how this altercation ended before it could escalate.

In a minute, they were walking away, deep in thought. Watching them retreat, I felt sad, for I could predict that the Babri issue, which had already divided communities, would now even tear relationships apart.

Conversely, the short exchange out in the corridor had convinced me of the immense powers of interpersonal communication. It dawned on me that my job in the telephone exchange was not just about keeping the lines buzzing and the phones ringing. It was also about hearing conflicting views, even on communitarian discord, and finding common ground for people even in the midst of social turmoil.

My mind then returned to my professional responsibilities. No matter what happened in the city in the coming days, the communication lines had to remain functional without fail. Purposefully, I started walking towards the Strowger Exchange, which is housed in the City Exchange building.

~

Before mobile phones, the Strowger exchanges were part of the backbone of India's telecommunications service. The technology was quite old and had an unusual origin story. It was developed by Almon Brown Strowger, an undertaker in Kansas, in the late 19th century. He was frustrated with local telephone operators, who, he suspected, had been diverting his business calls to a competitor. Thanks to Strowger the undertaker, human error or manipulation could no longer prevent people from connecting with each other; for now, calls could be routed and connected automatically. Stepping inside a Strowger Exchange was like walking into a bustling factory floor, where, instead of machines, there were racks upon racks of what we in telecommunications parlance call selectors. Inside the exchange, uni-selectors, group selectors, and final selectors whirred and clicked like clockwork, looking almost like sentient beings.

A uni-selector has multiple arms and rotating discs, which, when in action, resemble an octopus on steroids. These arms snatch incoming calls and direct them to the correct group selectors, the next level in the communication chain. Their finesse could earn the envy of even the most skilled juggler.

Group selectors are no slouches, either. They deftly juggle incoming calls, directing them to the final selectors with near-flawless accuracy. To those who understood what was going on, observing an exchange like this was like watching a symphony performed by metallic switches and relays. In this symphony, the final selectors are the grandmasters. They process every call, connect callers to receivers, and ensure that phone conversations in the city flow smoothly.

The exchange was a sight that day, almost comical in its whirring complexity. It was my duty to ensure that these machines ran like clockwork. After all, communications held the key to peace—even the slightest hiccup here could mean chaos in the city. But despite my sentimental love for classical analogue machinery, I had to admit that not all was well with the Strowger Exchanges. Its parts had started to behave like a mischievous child, constantly acting up and causing trouble. Often, the quality of material used to make the selectors was below the required standard. So, every other day, a new issue needed the attention of hordes of our technicians and engineers. From held-up calls to cross-talk to wrong numbers, the litany of problems seemed endless. And the excess billing! It was as if the machines had developed a mind of their own, much to the dismay of the customers.

The unfortunate engineers and technicians constantly dealt with the aftermath of the misbehaving Strowger Exchange. And yet, no matter how hard they tried, another issue always lurked around the corner. Sometimes, I felt as if the troika of selectors was conspiring against our customers and that it had banded together to wreak havoc on the system.

I drew a parallel from current events almost involuntarily, observing that despite all the frustrations and stresses, at least the technicians and engineers under my command were united in their battle against these stubborn machines. Besides, on the drive to work, I had vowed to myself that I would keep the phones in the city working at all costs, for I had seen the consequences of failure first-hand. That day, more than ever, every nut and bolt in Bhopal's government machinery needed seamless communication.

As I walked into the exchange thinking about all

this, Ramakant Mishra, a technician, stood to greet me.

'Good morning,' I said, glancing at the selectors as they moved up and down or rotated creakily, their cacophony filling the room, 'how many lines do we have up and running?'

'Sir, there are about 4,000 operational lines right now,' Mishra replied.

He sounded perturbed or distracted, and I wanted to probe the reason. Was it the usual concern for the ageing exchange, or was it the situation in Bhopal?

'It's a difficult situation,' I remarked casually. But his response revealed his innermost feelings.

'It certainly is, Sir,' he replied, nodding in agreement. Then he added, 'Everyone is trying to reach someone over the phone, and because of the load, the calls are not getting through.'

He pointed towards a bay of uni-selectors and said, 'Sir, do you see the selectors there, rotating simultaneously and then dropping? That bay serves Shahjahanabad, Ibrahimpura, Berasia Road, Taj-ul-Masjid, Sofia College and Noor Mahal. These localities are generating an abnormally high volume of traffic.'

I looked and nodded. I had passed through some of these areas not even a quarter of an hour ago.

'It means that either something has happened there, or people are planning something,' Mishra continued.

So that is why I had sensed tension pervaded the Strowger Exchange! The operators and technicians could actually pinpoint the exact points of possible conflict in the city. They could see the crescendo of calls mounting in some localities, slowly spreading to other places. I realised it would be a challenging day for those working in this building.

I looked at Mishra with compassion and silently appreciated his work. Despite the anarchy in the city, he was focused on his job. I knew I could count on him to get the job done, and I told him that.

'Thank you, Sir,' he replied, and I saw determination replace panic in his eyes.

After all these years working among the bays in which mechanical rotors and relays whirred continuously, I knew about the extraordinary skill and expertise required to keep the Strowger systems up and running. When there was an adverse situation, technicians like Mishra confronted a steep uphill climb.

Next, I turned to the new building in the City Exchange. It housed the E-10B Exchange, which also had the trunk exchanges, both automatic and manual, and special services, including a new computerised directory enquiry system.

To get to the new building, one had to cross a corridor, and an awkwardly built staircase had to be ascended and then descended. It was a modern structure with sleek lines that housed large racks filled with state-of-the-art equipment. The flashing lights and giant cables of this exchange seemed futuristic when compared with the mechanical Strowger Exchange next door.

The E-10B exchanges had been imported from France in the late eighties and early nineties, the early days of the telecommunications revolution in India. They were considered game-changers, thanks to their higher efficiency and advanced electronic technology. They were commissioned all over the country and later even manufactured here.

However, in the early nineties, many of us officials had not been trained to use these modern machines. I was not very well acquainted with the E-10B system, so I felt compelled to explore it that day. After all, no other officer had made it to the City Exchange, not even the Divisional Engineer, PK Jain, who was usually in charge of this exchange.

To my great surprise, the E-10B Exchange was empty of workers. Only one man, a worker, and a Junior Engineer, Manmohan Singh, were around. The worker, who had arrived on the night shift, had been unable to return home after his shift got over because of the rising incidents of violence on the streets, while Manmohan had managed to arrive on regular duty. The silence in the exchange was deafening.

'Could you tell me about the state of the exchange?' I addressed the Junior Engineer, not knowing how to begin.

Manmohan, a Sikh gentleman, looked up, revealing a face drawn with worry. I knew from his expression that now, minutes after having survived street-level rioters, I would face my first professional challenge of the day.

He straightened up and responded politely, 'Of course, Sir. There was an overload last night. Everyone in the old city, places like Idgah Hills, Kohefiza, and Lal Ghati, was trying to make calls simultaneously, leading to call failures. It would appear that there was a lot of tension in those areas.'

I peered at the rack displaying the to-and-fro calls and noticed the numerous flickering lights illuminating the room. 'What would happen if the situation worsened?' I asked, hoping for a more detailed response.

'The entire exchange could shut down. It's a critical situation. This exchange is not designed for such unprecedented loads. I'm doing everything possible to prevent a collapse,' Manmohan replied calmly.

However, he revealed that his bigger worry was the trunk automatic exchange that handles intercity calls. It is also run from the City Exchange building, and it connects Bhopal with the rest of the world. It had been acting up as calls were pouring into Bhopal from Delhi, Mumbai, Indore, Jabalpur, and Gwalior. If the trunk exchange failed, it could disrupt communication in the entire city. It meant that Bhopal might be cut off from the world. What is worse, any failure at the City Exchange would have a cascading effect on all other exchanges and could severely impact emergency services, too. It was a precarious situation.

When I heard the Junior Engineer's worries, I knew that the situation was far worse than I had anticipated. Since the demolition in Ayodhya, the events had taken everyone by surprise, not just in Bhopal but across the country. And our city, like the rest of the nation, was ill-prepared for the unrest that had erupted overnight.

Still, with skilled professionals like Manmohan at the helm, I hoped that our telephone systems would at least hold out and help us weather the storm.

Manmohan then rushed to answer the landline telephone, which had been ringing without a break. It was DK Gupta, the Chief General Manager, on the line, and he was looking for the Divisional Engineer. Gupta, whom we called CGM Gupta, had a towering personality accompanied by a voice that commanded attention. His long, flowing sidelocks added to his distinguished appearance.

He had a unique way of starting his sentences when he wanted to make a point—with the words 'bloody hell'—but he was more endearing than rude.

Despite his intimidating aura, I considered myself fortunate to work under his guidance. He recognised my hard work and frequently expressed his appreciation, even in writing. It was he who, despite the norm of allocating official vehicles only to Divisional Engineers in charge of outdoor plants, had approved the jeep for me, although I was in charge of an internal plant. In those days, an official vehicle was a privilege few officials had access to.

Back then, I often imagined Gupta as the tough hero in Bollywood films who always prevailed on the bad guys. With his signature bloody hells, he would bring the villains to justice in the most spectacular ways possible.

I picked up the phone and greeted him.

'Jain, what took you so long to answer my calls,' he demanded.

'Sir, this is Anupam here. PK Jain has yet to arrive,' I replied. Jain was the Divisional Engineer of the E-10B.

'Why the hell not? It is 12:30 in the afternoon,' roared Gupta, and I knew he would soon write a memo seeking an explanation from Jain.

'Sir, there is tumult in the city, and many roads are blocked. Maybe he is stuck,' I said to protect my colleague.

'But Anupam, how did you reach the exchange?' he asked in a softer voice.

I explained that the driver came in the official jeep to pick me up at my home and realised my mistake as soon as the words had left my mouth. During those days, official vehicles were not allowed to pick up officers from their residences. We were supposed to come to the workplace on our scooters and only then use government vehicles.

But CGM Gupta didn't seem to mind today, so I continued, telling him that I had been unaware of the troubles in the city when I had left my home that morning.

'What's the situation at the exchange?' the CGM then inquired, adding, 'The Communications Minister Rajesh Pilot-ji is in Saharanpur and I was talking to him this morning—but why the hell did our calls keep disconnecting? What is the situation at the exchange?' A hint of uncertainty coloured his tone, for he was aware of my limited expertise regarding the E-10B Exchange.

At this point, I refrained from telling him everything that had happened since morning—the dangerous drive to work, the mob outside the exchange building, the fires I had seen, and the slogan-shouting—but he had to know the crucial facts. So, I informed him that I was the only officer present on the premises, that there were only a few technicians and junior engineers other than me, and that the Trunk Exchange in E-10B was getting overloaded, which is why calls were getting disconnected.

'Okay, so now, managing the City Exchange is your responsibility,' he responded. 'Don't bother about the Arera Exchange; I will depute Chaturvedi there. Make sure that the service runs smoothly,' he added.

Trying to sound confident, I said, 'Yes, Sir. I will do my best.' Then, eager to reassure him and prevent Chaturvedi from entering the territory I was responsible for overseeing, I quickly added, 'Sir, I will manage the Arera Exchange, too.'

'Bloody hell! You focus only on the City Exchange, which is the most crucial,' he thundered.

'Yes, Sir. I understand,' I replied, trying to match his authoritative tone.

'You see, I just got a call from Nirmala, asking me

to be alert and to take care of our network,' Gupta said, leaving me to wonder who Nirmala was. 'She told me that there are a lot of clashes in the city and that the telephones must work efficiently to ensure law and order can be maintained,' he said.

It took me a moment to realise that he was referring to the Chief Secretary, the top bureaucrat of the state, Nirmala Buch. Gupta always addressed officers of other services by their first names.

'Keep me updated,' he said before ending the call. 'Yes, Sir,' I replied, catching myself nodding during the phone call.

I held on to the handset for a few seconds to ensure that the call had disconnected and then took a deep breath, feeling the weight of the responsibility on my shoulders. My mind raced through all the tasks I had lined up for the day. I knew I had to step up if I wanted to succeed in my new role as custodian of communications.

ये देश है वीर जवानों का, अलबेलों का मस्तानों का
इस देश का यारों क्या कहना, ये देश है दुनिया का गहना
यहाँ चौड़ी छाती वीरों की, यहाँ भोली शक्लें हीरों की...

Our country of brave soldiers, of carefree people
Friends, our country is the jewel of the world
The brave have broad chests here, and the heroes,
innocent faces...

CHAPTER TWO

Safe Haven

December 7, afternoon

The moment I stepped out of the new building, I saw Mustafa running towards me. The usually well-groomed fellow looked unkempt, almost white with fear.

'Mustafa, *sab theek toh hai?*' I asked if all was well.

He explained to me that his family was in danger and that he needed to leave right away to help them. His fear for his loved ones was writ large in his voice and face.

'Of course, please go to your family. Is there anything I can do to help?' I asked. Though I felt helpless, I wanted to offer support.

Mustafa nodded and, with an aadaab—the courteous salutation the last Nawab of Awadh, Wajid Ali Shah, introduced to honour Lucknow's secular fabric—rushed away. As I watched him go, concern for his safety and that of his family flooded over me. He was a good person and a reliable driver. Sometimes, I felt he was always by my side like a trusted lieutenant. I recalled what he had said while we drove to the exchange this morning, including protecting me no matter what. But it looked like today was my day to worry for his well-being and to pray that his family, too, would be okay.

~

Once again, I focussed on sorting out the mess in the City Exchange. I swiftly gathered all the employees for a meeting. There were just twenty-five on duty that day when there would have been 200 on regular days.

Each of them looked afraid and uncertain, wondering what would happen next and whether they could return home safely. The anxiety was understandable, given the disturbances brewing outside. I had to break it to them that they would have to stay on the premises all night to keep the phone lines running. I knew that if these personnel returned to their homes, they would not have been able to return to the exchange to work the next day!

I addressed them calmly, hoping to inspire confidence in everybody.

'Friends, I know that this is a difficult time, but I need your cooperation to ensure the safety of everyone here and to make sure the communication system works well,' I announced.

A murmur of agreement rose from within the modest assembly, and I could sense that they expected me to guide them.

'In the current situation, it's not advisable for you to return home as there are dangers of attacks by unruly elements. We will ask the next-door tent house to arrange our stay and meals. We will ensure your well-being as best as possible. Until the situation comes under control, your safety is our top priority. I hope you will understand the seriousness of our circumstances,' I said.

They heard me out with rapt attention and seemed reassured. I continued, 'I will also stay here with you and not return home. Together, we must maintain the communications system and stay in constant touch with the authorities. Our job is to align with the government's larger response effort.' The sense of relief among the workers when they heard that I, the seniormost officer, would not leave them alone, was perceptible. One employee whispered a joke to another: 'Sounds like it will be a picnic.' I couldn't resist beaming a broad smile at him.

As the employees began to disperse and return to their work, I noticed one group huddled together, murmuring amongst themselves. Did they have a concern that needed to be addressed? I approached them and inquired if they had something to say. One employee raised a concern. 'A structure on our exchange premises has been a point of dispute for a long time,' he said.

I looked at him, my curiosity aroused. 'What kind of structure?'

'A small one that some people believe is a temple, while others believe it to be a mazaar,' he replied. 'The authorities have declared that it is a disputed structure, but religious groups outside the exchange have been striving to take advantage of the dispute and play political football over it,' he said.

He had raised a serious concern. 'I see,' I said while a distant memory about the mazaar—a tomb-shrine typical to many parts of India—resurfaced. This employee had reminded me of a conversation long ago in which someone had warned me that a 'miniature Ram Mandir-Babri Masjid issue' was simmering within the City Exchange.

'How have you handled this situation so far?' I inquired, careful not to reveal my prior knowledge about this issue.

With a hint of pride, the man replied, 'Sir, the employees in the city exchange are almost equally distributed as Hindus and Muslims,' he said, 'but we are broad-minded and tolerant. We have kept the structure beyond the reach of outsiders and never allowed the issue to flare up.'

Impressed, I nodded in agreement. 'That's commendable,' I said. 'But why do you think this issue is relevant now?'

The employee looked worried. 'Sir, today everyone is feeling religiously charged,' he said.

In other words, he suspected that there could be an attempt by a mob to infiltrate the exchange premises to demolish this structure or proclaim it as a temple or mazaar.

'Since there are no security arrangements here, we are worried about our own safety, too,' he said.

His genuine concerns made me realise that ensuring food and accommodation was not enough to make the workers feel secure.

'Thank you for bringing this to my attention,' I said, adding, 'I will make security arrangements immediately to protect us all as well as the structure.'

For the second time that day, I confronted a critical situation in which time was of the essence. Back in my office, I felt my heart thumping as I dialled the number of Subhash Atre, the Superintendent of Police in Bhopal. But all I got was a constant busy tone. Minutes later, feeling quite frustrated, I knew I had to find another way to get in touch with him.

Not wasting time, I rushed back to the E-10B telephone exchange. I knew that there were protocols and procedures we must follow, but in today's crisis, there was no time to waste. I needed to get through to Police Superintendent Atre and fast.

I found Manmohan in the exchange and explained the situation to him. He would have to intrude into an ongoing call of the Superintendent of Police—something far from the ideal in normal times. I knew that barging into a police officer's call was a perilous affair, but those were not ordinary circumstances, and our City Exchange would be unsafe if I did not take this risk.

Desperate times call for desperate measures, but the Junior Engineer demurred. It took a stern look from me and my order in a slightly raised voice. 'We don't have time,' I urged.

Manmohan nodded and complied. It was a tense few minutes, but he managed to locate the correct call amidst the chaos of the telephone exchange and patched me through to the police superintendent's phone.

My unconventional step to protect myself and all those around me proved fortunately timed, for Subhash Atre's ongoing call had just finished and he was yet to answer the one that was making his phone instrument ring. As a result, the unknown caller and I heard his voice simultaneously. I immediately began to explain the primacy of my call.

'Subhash-ji, this is the Divisional Engineer in charge of the telephone exchange. I need your immediate attention,' I said.

'We have received information about possible disturbances in some parts of the city. We need your immediate action to ensure the safety of citizens,' I continued.

The unknown caller interrupted me at this point, but I quickly interjected. 'Sorry, Sir, but I need you to hang up the phone so that I can speak to the SP,' I said firmly. The caller hesitated before hanging up, allowing me to continue my conversation.

'I see—what more details do you have?' Atre asked unflinchingly.

I could hear the chatter on the police wireless in the background. There was constant talk about rapid outbreaks of violence.

'We have identified specific areas where tempers are running high, including Shahjahanabad, Ibrahimpura, Berasia Road, Taj-ul Masjid, Sofia College, Noor Mahal, and the Idgah Hills locality,' I replied nervously, passing on the information gathered by our technicians and junior engineers.

'Thank you,' said Atre, promising immediate action. He offered to connect the call to concerned police stations we could alert and said I could call him again if there were any further updates to share. I also heard him ask an assistant to connect him to the police station hotlines.

'I have one more request, Subhash-ji. We have reason to believe that there may be an intrusion into the City Exchange, and we need your help to ensure its safety,' I said with concern.

Atre listened carefully. 'What kind of threat are we talking about?' he then asked.

I explained everything I knew and said, 'I need you to deploy your forces at the City Exchange as soon as possible.'

It was vital to act quickly. Only timely steps could prevent harm to life and property at the exchange.

Atre offered a few words of praise and encouragement

at my initiative, and then said, 'Don't worry. I will send policemen to provide you with protection. Thank you for bringing all this to my attention, Mr...?' he said, pausing for my name.

'I am Anupam Shrivastava, Subhash-ji; nice speaking to you,' I said.

'Thanks, Mr Shrivastava, and let us remain in touch,' he said.

As I hung up the phone, Manmohan looked at me, still concerned but admiringly. 'Sir, that was incredible. You really took charge of the situation,' he said.

'Thanks, but we are not out of the woods yet. We still have work to ensure that communications remain uninterrupted and people feel safe.'

But I allowed myself to breathe a sigh of relief after this call. It had lifted my spirit, and I felt proud that our work would help the police in their effort to maintain law and order in our troubled city. To my further relief, the police responded promptly to my call for help as, in an hour or so, six policemen arrived at our doorstep, armed with sticks and batons to protect us from harm. When they entered my room, it was hard to ignore the worry and distress painted all over their faces. One of them saluted me, and the other said, 'We've been sent here, but we're feeling anxious ourselves. We don't know who will take care of our security.'

The third one swore in the name of a revered deity: '*Ganpati Bappa ki saugandh*, we want to do our duty, but we don't want to die doing it.'

'There are rioters out there who wanted to kill anyone in khaki. Today, in Jahangirabad, one constable was brutally assaulted by a mob, and we don't know if he'll survive,' said a constable.

Their words reminded me of the policemen I had seen being chased in Jahangirabad a few hours ago, and the thought that the circumstances had worsened made me shiver—it could have been Mustafa and me battling for our lives, not just the constable who faced assault.

It was difficult to accept that the police personnel who had arrived to secure us were feeling nervous and worried about their own security. However, after some thought, I decided to respect their concerns and allowed them to return to their police station for safety. But now, the City Exchange was at the mercy of God.

The situation in Bhopal was dire on that first day of the demolition of the Babri Masjid, and there was no sign that the situation would improve the next day. People were being brutally beaten and killed on the streets. The assailants were armed with knives, swords, and machetes. There were reports of widespread damage to properties across the city. Unfortunately, the police bore the brunt of the violence, as they were hugely outnumbered by the mobs.

As the police tried to bring order to the streets, they became an easy target of the same people they were trying to protect. The mobs redirected their anger and frustration towards the uniformed officials, who were often ill-equipped to deal with the utter collapse of law and order. The riots served as a tragic reminder of the deep-seated religious and cultural hostilities in India, which, though latent, still existed, not to mention the challenges faced by law enforcement officials in such a volatile environment. Therefore, the concerns expressed by the six police personnel sent to protect the exchange were genuine.

Consumed by troubling thoughts about our safety, I answered my phone as soon as it rang. It was Colonel Ramanujam, a friend who worked in the Indian Army. He often visited my office to use our STD phones to talk to his family in Kerala. Those days, long-distance calls were not only expensive but also unavailable on most phones. We, officers of the Telephone Department, were privileged to have STD facility on our phones and often shared it with others, especially the Army personnel.

The colonel had served in the Indian Peace Keeping Force in Sri Lanka from 1987 to 1990, after which it was withdrawn from its operations in Northern and Eastern Sri Lanka and renamed the 21st Corps. It became a quick-reaction force within the Indian Army, headquartered near Bhopal. In 2014, India even constructed a war memorial at Bhopal to honour the peace-keeping force.

'Hello, Colonel, how are you doing?' I asked.

'I'm doing well, thank you. How about you?' he replied. 'I called to enquire about your telephone exchange. Is everything running smoothly?' he asked.

'Yes, everything is fine,' I said sarcastically.

'Well, that's good to hear,' he said but ignored my sarcasm. 'I wouldn't want to miss my next visit to your office for a cup of tea and misuse the STD facility,' he joked.

I laughed. 'You know how to make me feel better, Colonel,' I said, feeling slightly relaxed.

'I'm glad, Boss. Now, let us get serious. How are you and your people holding up in all the chaos?' he asked.

'It has been a tough day, but we're managing,' I replied, 'the building and staff need security, but the police are unable to provide it.'

'OK, leave it to me. I'll send some soldiers to the exchange. They won't let anything happen to you or your team,' he assured me.

I couldn't believe my ears. 'Thank you so much, Colonel! You're a lifesaver!' I exclaimed.

He chuckled, 'I know, I know. Just doing my duty. Now, take care. We'll talk soon.'

Within an hour, as I looked out of the window, I saw three soldiers in olive green uniforms holding automatic weapons walking past. Very soon, they were standing in my office.

The soldiers stood tall in their uniforms, their solid build reflecting their physical prowess and training. The sleek, black automatic weapons in their arms looked ready to face any challenge that came their way. Their faces showed unshakeable determination. A voice in my head muttered, could they be outnumbered by any mob? As if reading my thoughts, one of them said, 'Sir, we are enough to face any threat. Trust us.'

His firm reassurance gave me a glimmer of hope. I nodded silently, grateful for the bravery and determination of these soldiers. They headed towards the main entrance of the exchange as I prayed for their safety and success, silently thanking Col Ramanujam for his timely help.

December 7, 1992, had been a long and hectic day. Still at my desk in the evening, I pored over some OCHLA reports from the E-10B exchange. These are outgoing call handling and logging arrangement reports, which record all calls from a telephone exchange. These reports are generated automatically by the exchange and contain details such as the numbers called, call durations, the time and date of calls, and other related technical details.

OCHLA reports are important to track and monitor the performance of an exchange. They could also be used for billing purposes. In addition, they can have important security uses, as they provide a record of calls made during a particular period, which could help investigate any incident or threat. I had no prior experience reading these reports, although I had learned about them during my training sessions. Now, I wanted to read them so that the junior engineers and technicians could take timely action to maintain the exchange's communication lines.

Consumed by work, I lost track of the time. I had been working tirelessly, not realising how late it was, until someone suddenly switched on the lights in the room. I looked up, and saw the office peon, Dori Lal. His small gesture made me realise that even in the midst of chaos, we were supporting each other.

Suddenly, the red telephone to the left of my table rang out. Without shifting my attention from the reports I had been examining, I extended my hand and answered the call. It was Gokul Singh, my immediate boss, a real taskmaster. He had a medium build, distinguished by his thick, white hair and clean-shaven face. He also possessed exceptional leadership skills, consistently supported his team, and inspired it to surpass its limits. His expectations of me were always high.

Renowned for his unwavering work ethic, Singh often arrived early and departed late from the office, occasionally burning midnight oil alongside his subordinates. He was held in high regard, and employees frequently sought his guidance on both personal and professional matters.

Singh was an actual role model for his team. Beneath his serious demeanour, he possessed a razor-sharp wit and an infectious sense of humour that could lift the weakest spirit. During weekends, he organised team-building dinners and outings, occasionally spiced up with a few drinks to help his team unwind. His quick wit endeared him to everyone around him. He also set the right example with his unwavering obedience to his superior, CGM Gupta.

'Hey Anupam, how's it going?' he asked cheerfully.

'Good morning, eh, good evening, Sir,' I muttered as I silently reprimanded myself for losing track of time again.

It had been a long, chaotic day, and my mind was clearly not as sharp as it should be.

'I'm doing fine, Sir, just analysing the OCHLA report,' I quickly added.

My boss teased me with a light-hearted chuckle. 'Do you even know what that is?' he joked, converting his playful chuckle into full-blown laughter.

I laughed, too, 'Yes, Sir, I do. It's the telecom traffic report, remember?'

Singh continued, 'Oh, I see. Just making sure you're not analysing the stock market report or something.'

We laughed again, and I felt grateful for having such a supportive boss.

But in the next moment, his tone changed, and as if he had suddenly recalled the gravity of the situation, he said in a dead-serious tone, 'Anupam, what is the situation in the City Exchange? Are you keeping things together?' he asked, sounding concerned.

I gave him a brief update on our efforts to keep things running smoothly. 'Everything is under control. We're working hard and managing to keep the telephone lines up and running. The exchanges are working well,' I said. 'And, Sir, in the morning, CGM Gupta called me while I was visiting the E-10B Exchange, inquiring about why his call with the Communications Minister had dropped. When I analysed the problem through the OCHLA reports, I discovered that the issue lay not on our side but with Saharanpur. I spoke with the DE in charge there, RM Agarwal, and requested him to investigate the concerns,' I added with a hint of pride in my voice.

'That is great to hear!' he exclaimed, 'Anupam, I always knew you had it in you to handle a tough situation. You're a natural leader.'

'Thank you, Sir, I appreciate your support. Today, we will sleep in the exchange building to keep things running. We've arranged for food and other necessities. We're also working in shifts to ensure no break in our service,' I reported.

Singh listened carefully and then responded with just a long, thoughtful 'hmm'. In a moment, he said, 'Do you know, Anupam, that my friend, the Collector of Bhopal MA Khan, called me just an hour ago? The poor chap was very distressed. He said that everyone is looking at him with suspicion, Hindus and Muslims alike. He was worried that he would be transferred soon.'

I felt sorry for Collector Khan's woes.

Singh continued, 'How's the situation outside the exchange? Are the riots ongoing in the old city?'

'Yes, Sir, rioting is also being reported at many places around the City Exchange building. But we're doing our best to keep things going,' I replied.

'And, Sir, the Army is helping us. Three soldiers sent by Col Ramanujam are a huge help. They are stationed outside our building, standing almost like statues, but fully alert and with their weapons. It's given us all a sense of relief and security in this chaos,' I said.

Singh said, 'Good job, Anupam. Keep up the good work. I'll be in touch.' Then he quickly added, 'Anupam, you're doing all the hard work. I'm just giving you a pep talk and making sure you don't fall asleep at your desk.' As he ended the call with another joke, I chuckled, too.

His humour could make the most stressful situation bearable, I thought. So here we were, working round the clock while angry hordes roamed around, ravaging the streets of Bhopal.

My team and I worked away, allaying our collective fears by reminding ourselves of the importance of our duties when the city seemed to have turned dystopian. We were a tight-knit team and had arranged for essential supplies in advance and called a wedding caterer to prepare our meals. The cooks were also asked to sleep in the exchange premises to ensure that every employee was well-fed, including those who came in later that day or the next.

Feeling relaxed after the call with my boss, I decided to take another round of the City Exchange. I started at the Strowger Exchange, then moved towards the E-10B Exchange. Everywhere, I saw the staff working meticulously on their tasks. Next, I went to the trunk exchange, where I was pleased to see the team responsible for maintaining the lines doing an excellent job. They had left no significant issues to be addressed by me. The lights there blinked in a steady, rhythmic pattern, indicating that the long-distance calls were flowing smoothly from and to Bhopal. The sight of those twinkling lights felt therapeutic, for they were functioning seamlessly despite everything going on in the city and our hearts. A gentle smile spread over my face. It was a small victory, but it felt like a big one at that moment.

As I turned to leave, I noticed a couple of technicians in a corner, bent over a console. I walked over and gave them a collective pat on their backs with one arm. 'Good job,' I said, my voice filled with gratitude. The technicians' faces lit up. Their warm smiles conveyed to me their sincere acknowledgment.

Next, I went to the microwave building, where I saw a few technicians working to ensure that the signal end of telecommunications was transmitting uninterrupted. I then visited the battery plant, which was filled with a perpetual hum and the unmistakable pungent smell of acid. That odour was so overpowering that it made my nose twitch, and I knew that a bitter taste would linger in my mouth after this inspection. The stacks of batteries in this plant were the lifeline of the entire exchange. If the power were to go off, they would provide uninterrupted power supply to the switches and computers.

Every exchange needed a battery plant, a power plant, and even a diesel generator for backup power. The City Exchange also had an 11-kilovolt transformer and other electrical systems, which had to be carefully maintained. Each of these systems—the power plant, the generator room, and the 11 KV transformer room—was always lively with its own noises, especially the buzz and hum of the Voltmeter and Ammeter needles swinging back and forth against their plain displays. A lone technician wearing large, framed spectacles that continuously slipped off his nose sat at his desk at the battery plant. He was busily entering readings in a logbook.

'His chair needs repair,' I noted, mentally reprimanding the officer in charge of supplies, who was not around.

I took a deep breath of satisfaction as the hum of the power and battery plants was a concert to my ears. It meant that the selectors were rising and falling in the Strowger Exchange and that the lights in the trunk exchange room were flickering, which meant long-distance calls were flowing smoothly.

Relieved, I returned to my office to find that Dori Lal had set the table for dinner. The aroma of freshly cooked food wafting through the air made me realise how hungry I was. The table had been neatly arranged with plates and bowls filled with a culinary assortment. I saw chapatis, rice, mixed vegetables, and a bowl of dal. A plate of crisp papad and fresh salad was on the side. Curiously, a covered bowl was placed on a side table. Dori Lal waited for me to take a seat, a welcoming smile on his face. He was probably confident that his efforts to make my dinner as comfortable as possible would succeed. The table showed that it had been set with care. The bone China plates and bowls were spotless.

I took a moment to thank Dori Lal for the effort he had put into this meal, knowing that it would mean a lot to him. Then, I sat down to enjoy the food. First, I lifted the lid off the covered bowl. A delectable meat dish was inside. Dori Lal, now standing by my side, looked worried and frowned.

'Sir, this dish was sent by Ms Ayesha Aziz,' he said guardedly. 'Are you sure it's safe to eat this? With everything going on...'

Ayesha, a middle-aged Muslim woman who took care of my office with great proficiency—her husband worked as an operator in the City Exchange—had brought the dish for me. But with the Hindu-Muslim riots tearing apart the city, a palpable trust deficit had risen between its residents.

Cutting Dori Lal off, I reassured him that this was a goodwill gesture. 'It would be rude not to eat it. Besides, I trust her,' I said.

All through dinner, my thoughts wandered around the events that had led to our unfortunate situation. Resentments that had been simmering for a long time had boiled over after the demolition of the Babri

Masjid. The atmosphere was charged with mistrust and fear. However, I was determined not to let the situation cloud my judgement and affect my relationships with members of other faiths.

~

After the sumptuous meal, I washed my hands and found Dori Lal standing by my side, holding a white towel. I took it from him and wiped my hands. He told me there had been a few calls from my family while I had been inspecting the exchange. I realised that I had forgotten to call home all day.

Immediately, I dialled my home number. I felt homesick at the thought of being away for an indefinite period from my wife and children. When my wife answered the phone, I could hear Ankit and Mohit chattering in the background; their innocent voices were a comforting contrast to the outside world.

'Hi,' I said, 'it's me. How are you and the boys?'

'Hello?' she said and then, after recognising my voice, 'we're doing okay, but how are you? Are you safe?' Lots of concern coupled with annoyance were mixed up in the tone of her voice.

'Yes, I'm fine,' I said, realising that I had been negligent towards my duties as father and husband. I should have called home in the morning and informed my wife and my parents that I had reached the office safe and sound.

'I'm staying overnight at the exchange just to be safe and to ensure that the employees also can stay here and maintain the communications facility,' I told her.

'Do you have to?' she asked, raising her voice a bit. By now, she was surrounded by the clamour of the children. 'Is it Papa?' I could hear Ankit's voice. 'I want to talk to him,' he demanded.

Immediately, my younger son Mohit's voice also interrupted. 'Papa, when are you coming home? We miss you!'

'Why do you have to stay there?' my elder son Ankit's voice chimed in from the background as he took the phone from his mother's hand.

'Because there's trouble in the city right now,' I explained. 'But don't worry, everything will be fine.'

'What kind of trouble?' Mohit asked, taking the phone from his elder brother's hand.

'Some people are fighting, but the army and police are taking care of it,' I said reassuringly.

'But why are they fighting, Papa?' Ankit asked, taking the phone back. I could almost see their little tussle for my attention and the phone's receiver.

'It's a long story, *beta*,' I said. 'It's just some people being angry with each other,' I said. 'But don't worry about it right now. Just know that I'm doing my duty, and I'll be home soon.'

'What's their problem?' Ankit persisted. 'What's happened to their senses?' He sounded mature, way beyond his age.

I held back my words momentarily, trying to figure out how to explain the crisis to such little children.

'Well, some people are fighting and causing trouble over something that has happened in another part of the country. But don't worry, people are there to protect you, and we are all safe.'

'But why can't you come home, Papa?' Mohit whined.

'Because it's unsafe right now, and I have to ensure that the phones keep working,' I repeated. 'I promise that I'll come home as soon as things settle down. And then I will tell you that story,' I said, trying to lighten the mood.

'Chho She, Ba She and Ba Ba She' was my favourite story to tell my children and I had mentioned it to little Mohit to calm him down. It was the one in which Small Lion was my younger son, Big Lion was my elder son, and Very Big Lion was me. The three of us would go into the jungle to hunt and bring food, and the lioness at home, my wife, would cook for us all. My promise to tell him the story again worked wonders, for Mohit relaxed immediately. This bedtime story was repeated almost every night with the children cuddling up on either side of me. They would fall asleep listening to it, or, sometimes, I would doze off. My voice would gradually droop, and they would try to keep me awake.

'Be good to your mom and everybody else, okay?' I said. I could almost see Mohit and Ankit's faces on the other end of the phone line. Hopefully, I had allayed some of their fears.

'Okay, Papa,' both shouted in unison, adding, '*lo, Mummy se baat karo.*' With that, they handed the phone back to my wife and returned to playing their indoor games.

'Papa is worried about you. He keeps asking if we've heard from you,' my wife said, returning to the receiver. 'He is very concerned about the situation in town,' she said, a quiver in her voice. 'He's taken his rifle and 12-bore out of the loft and cleaned them. He's kept them ready, "just in case". He tested the rifle in the afternoon, firing a few blanks into the air.'

I felt a knot forming in my stomach. My wife was talking about my father, NP Shrivastava, who was not one to take such measures lightly. I knew that he must be genuinely concerned about the riots and the safety of the family. Although we lived in a safe area and most of the rioting so far was confined to old Bhopal, the panic was spreading.

'How are Mummy and Bobby?' I asked, and now even my voice was shaking a bit from worry. Bobby is my younger brother.

'Yes, both are fine,' my wife replied. 'Mummy is very worried about you. She keeps asking if you've eaten and whether you're staying safe.'

I sighed, feeling guilty about my mother's worries. I knew my decision to stay at the exchange was the right one, but it was not proving easy for my family to digest. I was touched by my mother's spot-on instinct, as she was always focussed on whether her son had eaten or not. But I didn't know what else to say except 'Tell her I'm fine'. Trying to convince my wife more than my mother, I added, 'I ate at the office, so ask her not to worry about me.'

'I will,' she said, but then she had to convey to me what Bobby had been up to. 'Bobby is very worked up about the riots,' she said with misgiving apparent in her voice. According to my wife, my brother had been collecting stones and glass bottles all day and had stocked them on the terrace. He believed fighting back with these items was the only way to protect our home if it came under attack. 'He plans to stay up there all night to keep watch and guard our house,' she continued.

I let out a heavy sigh. 'It is silly of Bobby to get worked up,' I said. 'We live in a peaceful area, and there is no threat there. He should focus on keeping himself and our family safe by staying calm, not seeking revenge or causing harm,' I added. My wife agreed, 'I've told him the same thing, but he is so angry about what's happening in the city that he will not listen to reason. I hope he returns to his senses soon.'

I knew that she herself wanted to ask if they were all safe in the neighbourhood. And I tried to ease her doubts, 'Don't worry, we are all safe,' I said firmly, 'tell Bobby to get off the roof. We must stay calm and united.'

'And have you really eaten?' she asked again.

'Yes, yes,' I replied. 'Okay then, good night and

take care,' I said, ending the conversation.

'Good night,' she replied. I imagined her, standing next to the telephone, misty-eyed. We held our phones in silence for ten seconds, and only when I heard the 'tarrrrrrrr' of the dial tone, followed by the 'tut-tut-tut' tone of the Strowger Exchange, did I hang up.

I still felt guilty for being away from my family during this trying time. My wife was my pillar of strength. She always comforted me, believing everything would eventually be alright and that I should always trust God. My children, on the other hand, couldn't comprehend why I had to stay away from home, the nature of my responsibilities, or why there was rioting in our city.

My mother was a typical Indian mother, mainly preoccupied with her children's meals. Food was her primary way to convey love and affection. She worried about the well-being of her children and wanted to ensure our safety. I was a grown man, but she viewed me as her small child, and so, naturally, she fretted even more about the dangers of this abnormal situation.

On the other hand, my father had been a dedicated government servant. He had joined the irrigation department in the fifties when junior engineers like him commuted for hours daily on bicycles, often going into dacoit-infested areas to supervise the newly independent nation's brand-new network of irrigation canals. He had instilled in me the virtues of hard work and dedication. He had always taken great pride in his work and raised me to follow in his footsteps, emphasising service and bringing a positive change in the world. But that day, he was anxious about the violence and its impact on the society he had devoted his life to serving.

And then there was Bobby, who seemed to believe that retaliation would quell the troubles in our city. He would always tell me, 'I strongly believe that we Hindus are too timid, and must not tolerate provocations!' Though my family had tried to reason with him in the present circumstances, especially by explaining that violence begets more violence and that peace was the only way to stop violence, he was angry and wanted to take matters into his own hands. By no means was Bobby violent—but he believed he would exert vengeance if attacked. What the family found hard to convince him about was that the perception of threat in our posh locality was minimal. And, what he also did not understand was that physical aggression would not come as naturally to him as his pride made him believe.

~

The rest of the first day in the office passed uneventfully and at night, I lay on the sofa under a duvet provided by the tent house. I could hear people shouting Allah-hu-Akbar and Jai Shri Ram outside the exchange. I tried to block the deafening sounds of the violence.

These two slogans were competing, trying to outdo one another in volume and intensity. They seemed to be waging a war for dominance, each asserting its superiority over the other in turns. It was a battle of religious ideologies that had spilt onto the streets. Such conflicts between belief systems, doctrines, and interpretations of religion could leave a trail of destruction. Now and then, the shouting would get louder and seemed to come from just outside the window, making me jump in fright. At night, even noises from afar seem to arise in close proximity. But as the night of December 7 progressed, the slogans and cries intensified, as if they were tearing apart the very fabric of society. The office windows had been securely shut, and the doors had been bolted, yet I felt a malevolent energy seeping into the room.

Amidst the slogan-shouting, there were cries of pain and anguish from those caught up in the violence. The sounds of police sirens, of running feet and screams, and the heavy boots of the army marching down the streets seemed to add to the pandemonium. It was a night I would never forget, the kind that makes you wonder if the world will ever be at peace again.

With a silent prayer for peace, night enveloped me, and I finally closed my eyes. Slowly, the competing phrases echoing outside were drowned out by the safety provided by my office's four walls.

हिंदू मुस्लिम सिख ईसाई, आपस में हैं भाई-भाई
भारत मां की गोद के पाले, आज़ादी के सब शैदाई
जागो, जागो, भारत के रहने वालों
जागो, हुआ सवेरा

Hindu, Muslim, Sikh, Christian, bound in brotherhood
Nurtured in Mother India's lap, where freedom finds its grace
Awaken, awaken, O dwellers of India's land
Awaken, for the morning has dawned, resolute and grand.

CHAPTER THREE

Sense and Senselessness

December 8, morning

The next day when I woke up at around 8 a.m., the sunlight had cast a golden hue outside my office window. When I looked out, the streets were deserted, and, surprisingly, there was no trace left of the carnage that had kept me awake for a good part of the night. At a distance, a loudspeaker blared a song from a 1940s Hindi movie that preached about harmony and brotherhood.

I walked out of my office and approached the main gate of the City Exchange. The big iron gate was a formidable structure with an air of having been on guard for centuries. It was at least nine feet tall and twelve feet wide with thick, rusted iron bars that had been painted over and over again, the old paint marks crisscrossing the newer layers to form a rugged grid.

The door was studded with metal bolts and locks,

giving the impression that it could withstand a huge amount of force. Its hinges creaked whenever it was opened, adding to its ominous appearance. It was a symbol of security and protection—and one had to feel at least a little safe behind this imposing door.

The soldier from the Indian Army had stood guard at the gate through the night. He stood at attention when he saw me and saluted as I approached, his boots making a sharp sound. I wondered how gritty the man was and how he had managed to stay awake and alert all night in such cold weather. I felt gratitude for him having kept us and the exchange building safe.

I stepped out into the street. Surprisingly, I saw nothing in the surroundings to even suggest that hoardes of rioters had trampled all over this area last night. It was as if the previous night's events had been a bad dream or a figment of my imagination—never a reality.

Feeling bolder, I walked further down the street to near the loudspeaker playing the song about social and religious harmony. The music got louder as the song reached its last stanza.

टूटे हुए दिलों को तुम आपस में जोड़ दो
झगडे तमाम वक़्त की नदी में छोड़ दो
जागो, जागो, जागो, भारत के रहने वालो
जागो, हुआ सवेरा

(Mend the broken hearts, let unity prevail
Dispose the quarrels, let the river of time sail

Awaken, arise, O dwellers of India's land
Awaken, for the morning has dawned, serene and
grand.)

It was a song from the Hindi movie, *Bhai* (Brother), which was conceived fifty years ago. It had a scary resonance with the present day as if the city of Bhopal had been plunged into the same darkness that had engulfed India during the horrors of the 1940s.

I walked on, towards Lal Ghati and then to the District Collector's office, where I noticed some signs that betrayed the previous night's violence. There was broken glass and other debris littering the street in front of the exchange, which was on the busy Bhopal-Sehore-Indore highway. There were also scorch marks on some buildings. It was clear that some violence had spilt from the confines of the old city the previous night. A small crowd of people stood nearby, looking unnerved. They appeared to be slum-dwellers and spoke in hushed tones as if afraid that the violence might erupt again at any moment.

Seeing those scared men bunched up in a corner on a cold December morning, I felt an instant unease about how communitarianism tramples on those who have no interest in the glories or the injustices of the past. The immediate present is all they are concerned about, and the next meal is all they hope for. Disheartened by the sight of the intimidated spirits of those men, I walked back to the exchange building at a quick pace.

Venturing out had been a futile attempt to shake off the unease that had precipitated within me.

There seemed to be a temporary halt to violence, but the air seemed pregnant with uncertainty. The city was holding its breath, waiting for something to happen. I hoped that it was something that would bring hope and heal the physical and psychological scars inflicted over the last 48 hours.

I now had the feeling that our society needed to make greater efforts to understand the complexities of identity conflicts, which lead to periodic violent outbursts in which our most vulnerable suffer the most. With this thought buzzing in my head, I hurriedly freshened up in the restroom attached to my office, grateful for the bucket of hot water that ever-dependable Dori Lal had brought for me.

~

Next, I mentally prepared myself for the day ahead. Dori Lal arrived promptly, carrying a steaming cup of tea, ensuring a comforting start to my day. Relishing the hot tea made me realise that simple comforts become a luxury when normalcy is thrown out of gear. I headed for my office table, ready to take on the tasks that awaited me. Within minutes, the engineers, technicians and other staff members trickled into my office. And in no time, the silence of the morning was replaced with loud, animated conversations, as everyone wanted to share the latest news and updates they had received from their families at night.

Rakesh Sharma, an operator from the trunk exchange, aged about thirty years, said with concern, 'Sir, last night, my father witnessed a distressing scene from our terrace. He saw a group of rioters setting fire to several shops. The flames were so intense that it sent a wave of terror through the neighbourhood.'

He quickly added, 'Sir, what's even more alarming is that despite the restrictions imposed under Section 144 on more than four people gathering in one place throughout the city, there seemed to be a severe lack of police personnel to enforce it.'

The room fell into a momentary silence.

Another junior telecom officer, Soheil Khan, the only Muslim who had managed to make it to work that day, also spoke up with a hint of anxiety, 'Sir, I could hear gunshots from my window last night. It felt like a war zone out there. The police conducted a frantic search of our neighbour's house, suspecting that he had firearms.'

Soheil's words seemed to float in the air. Nobody in the room seemed to possess the ability to catch them and comprehend his experience. We were all subdued by these personal accounts of the riots.

Another employee, Rajkumar, a technician in his early forties from the Strowger Exchange, interjected tremulously, 'Sir, my younger brother was returning from the market when he encountered a group of bearded men wearing skull caps. They were armed with sticks and hurling stones, shouting slogans and vandalising shops. It was a terrifying sight straight from a nightmare. My brother was gripped with fear for his life.'

Atma Ram, the diligent power plant cleaner, joined the conversation with a sombre tone, 'Sir, while I was cleaning the battery last night, I heard religious chants and hateful exchanges between people from different communities. Curiosity got the better of me, and I climbed to the top of the exchange building and saw a sight straight out of a horror movie. People were running in panic, desperately seeking safety, while police struggled to take control of the deteriorating situation. Meanwhile, loudspeakers were broadcasting religious slogans and hateful exchanges between communities.'

His words painted a vivid picture of the chaos that had kept me awake last night. Dori Lal stood by attentively, waiting to retrieve my empty teacup. He, too, couldn't contain his emotions any longer. He spoke up, sharing his ordeal, '*Saheb, humari jhuggi hai Apsara talkies kay baju me, jala diye kal. Pata nahi hamara ghar bacha ki nahi...*' The woes he narrated were soul-shaking—his family lived in a hut in a settlement behind the Apsara theatre that had been burnt down the previous night. He did not know if his house and family had survived the attack.

Dori Lal's eyes welled up with tears, reflecting the anguish of the fear and uncertainty that had befallen him. Without saying another word, he quickly departed the room, choosing to grieve in solitude.

As I listened to the officers and staff recount their experiences from the previous night, I felt a surge of emotions. It was evident that the city's wounds would need plenty of time to heal if they ever could. Uncertainty hung in the air, asking the haunting question: would normalcy return, or has a new normal been established?

Without thinking, I began, 'The worst part was that in Pakistan...' But I caught myself in the middle of my ill-conceived sentence. Before the words could leave my mouth, I realised my mistake. I wanted to convey the distressing news that I had heard from a colleague at the Arera Exchange that thirty or thirty-five temples had been destroyed in Pakistan on the previous day. But I realised the need for caution in fragile circumstances. Such news has the propensity to ignite both the gullible and the angry.

But the mixed expressions in the eyes of the staff had also made me acutely aware of the pull of contradictory emotions that they were grappling with—fear on the one hand, and also religious fervour on the other. As I was responsible for their safety and that of their families, I knew that we must stand together despite the prevailing conflict and first find a way to peace within our exchange.

'Last night was traumatic for all of us,' I began, ending the discussion on everybody's suffering. 'It's crucial that we keep supporting one another even in these challenging times. Let us ensure that we keep the phone lines working so people can stay in touch with their loved ones. Our primary responsibility is to assist the law enforcement authorities in their duties. And let us not forget, we should not believe or justify rumours,' I said. I hoped to convey the bigger picture of the situation and the larger purpose served by our collective capacities.

I looked at each of them, hoping I had adequately conveyed the importance of our duties to them. 'Let us restore peace in our hearts. Let that be our first goal,' I said. I knew the employees could relate to the life stories of inspiring figures, so I mentioned Henry Ford, the iconic industrialist, reminding them of what he once said, 'Coming together is a beginning, keeping together is progress, working together is success.'

I let these words sink in.

'We are a team, and, guided by a higher force, we have proven our commitment to unity. This unity will undoubtedly bring us success if we proceed with a shared purpose,' I said.

Finally, the staff nodded in agreement, and I saw a sense of determination awaken in their eyes. My little pep-talk restored their sense of purpose, a first step towards restoring normalcy. As the discussion wrapped up, a thought crossed my mind: it's so easy to get swept up in rumours when we are afraid, but clear communication still retains its power to maintain peace and stability. While the employees filed back to their respective workstations, I hoped they did so with a renewed pride in their contribution to preventing the rioting from escalating.

~

The day wore on with me glued to my desk, delving deeper into the OCHLA reports. By now, it was obvious that the violence in Bhopal had become quite severe. I scribbled notes and observations from other reports meant to track networks in my leather-bound notebook. All the time, my mind raced to keep up with the deluge of information I had to process. I prepared a small set of instructions for the technicians and junior engineers.

All day long, the telephone on my desk rang incessantly, each call demanding my attention and expertise in dealing with the extraordinary situation. As the hours passed, my mind felt better prepared to adapt to the situation. I answered each call with a cool, professional demeanour—an ability that seemed to have developed naturally. It made me wonder if the human spirit is stronger than we understand. My rationality transcended my fears, and I felt it in my voice, which had also developed confidence and authority.

Later in the afternoon, as the sun began to sink in the sky and the shadows lengthened outside my office, I finally had a moment to catch my breath.

I leaned back, still seated on my chair, took a deep breath, and finally let my eyes drift closed, just for a moment. My thoughts turned to the conversations with Col Ramanujan and Atre, the Superintendent of Police. I replayed their words in my mind, searching for new insights or revelations on the sensitive situation in Bhopal.

But before I could dive too deep into my ruminations, my focus was pulled back by a noise outside my door. Instinctively, I dismissed the commotion as the usual hustle and bustle of a workplace, but the sounds of very many footsteps running towards my room made me alert. I sat up straight. Tucking away my notebook and smoothening my shirt, I prepared to face whatever lay on the other side.

In moments, several of my employees, their faces etched with fear and anger, stood outside my office door. They seemed to want to tell me something but were too terrified—or excited—to speak. 'What's going on?' I asked, rising from my seat and walking towards them.

One of them mustered the courage to speak. 'Sir, we have some terrible news. Last night, Aziz Ahmad was shot dead by police.'

I absorbed the shocking news with difficulty. It took me several seconds to retrieve Aziz's image from memory. The weight of his untimely passing immediately weighed heavily on my heart. I slumped onto the nearby sofa, overcome by shock. My employees gathered around me, their expressions reflecting my feelings; a mix of disbelief and sorrow.

Aziz, with his slender frame and slight resemblance to the legendary American President, Abraham Lincoln, appeared unimposing at first glance. However, it was his soft-spoken nature and gentle demeanour that truly defined him. His colleagues held him in high regard, considering him a mentor and a dear friend. His dedication and commitment to work was evident throughout his tenure as an operator in the directory enquiry section, '197'. Despite his unassuming appearance, he consistently displayed strong work ethics, which left a lasting impression on those who worked with him. His loss was devastating, and I knew that he would be deeply missed.

Aziz and I were hierarchically apart within the organisation, but we had shared a significant professional experience while collaborating on a prestigious and time-sensitive project.

Just then, Uttam, the union leader, entered. He was well-known, both for his wisdom and distinguished appearance. He had thick white hair and was always dressed in a white kurta-pyjama. His arrival filled the room with silence. Everybody who had gathered around me respectfully made way for him, and he joined me on the sofa.

'Hello, Sir,' he began. 'I heard the distressing news about Aziz Ahmad's demise. It is an immense loss,' he began.

'Yes,' I replied. 'I still can't believe it. It's very tragic.'

Uttam's face displayed concern as he continued, 'Sir, I have heard an accusation. It is that Aziz was rioting, which led to the tragic police encounter. Some say, the police believe that he killed three people in the riots. They knocked on his door right after a skirmish, and, as he stepped out, shot him fatally at close range.'

My jaw dropped in disbelief when I heard this information. 'But it makes no sense,' I blurted. 'Aziz was a religious man, known for his kindness and gentleness. I can't imagine him ever being violent, let alone rioting!'

Uttam nodded. 'Indeed, Sir,' he concurred, sadness peeping through his eyes as he fell silent for a long time.

For a fleeting second, I wondered if the sagacious Uttam was reflecting on the argument he and Aziz had had in the corridor the previous day. Until I had intervened, neither of them had been acting in character. Then, Uttam spoke up rather philosophically. 'It is a paradox. Religious prejudice can take hold of anyone, and especially when influential leaders are involved, the human psyche can get deeply impacted. People can then do unimaginable things,' he said.

'I know people can do the unimaginable,' I said, sighing heavily. 'But to think that Aziz, who worked so hard and was so dedicated to his job, could do such things and also that he has been taken away from us, is hard to fathom,' I added.

Uttam then reminded me of the project that Aziz and I had worked on together. He said, 'Aziz was a gem. Meticulous and committed to perfection. I remember you told us how impressed MD Rathore was by his work on the Pune project. He had even personally told CGM Gupta Sir how exceptional Aziz was.'

Of course I remembered, I nodded in response. The project in Pune involved publishing a directory with Yellow Pages tailored for the city of Bhopal for 1992-93. It held great importance to our organisation and customers. It was the brainchild of CGM Gupta, my trailblazer of a boss who had guided our team on that ambitious mission. We had decided to introduce unheard-of features in the directory for that time, such as bold entries, double entries, and strategically placed boxed advertisements alongside names and numbers.

Besides, the project had generated additional revenue for our organisation. We could not only distribute the telephone directory to our customers free of charge, we also sold advertising space in its pages. The Rathore whom Uttam had referred to was Ashok Rathore, the Managing Director of a publishing firm, Sesa Seat Information Systems Limited, which had printed the directory. It had secured the printing contract through a competitive bidding process. It was a solid company, backed by Sesa Goa Pvt Limited, which held a majority stake of sixty per cent, while an Italian company held the remaining forty per cent.

I easily recalled Rathore, who was highly impressed by Aziz, and with whom I had closely interacted during the publication process. The partnership with his company had given our organisation access to a reputed and expert printing and distribution service, while the additional revenue generated from the Yellow Pages had sweetened the arrangement for our organisation and customers. Each time we met, Rathore would remark on Aziz's commitment, attention to detail, and outstanding work ethic. The lasting impression Aziz had made on him was heartening. After all, it affirmed the dedication and high quality of one of our organisation's staffers.

Aziz and I went on several trips to Pune while planning and executing this project. We meticulously proofread the directory, ensuring its accuracy and quality. It was a challenging task, and, while overseeing the project, I saw how effective and efficient he was at work.

These memories reaffirmed my belief that religious bigotry was senseless and wrought devastating consequences on individuals and communities. The loss of Aziz was also a stark reminder of the destructive power of prejudice and the urgent need for harmony and understanding in our city. Snapping out of the past, I said to Uttam, 'Aziz took immense pride in his work, and it showed. It's a shame that his life was cut short.'

At this point, another troubling memory came to my mind, and I decided to share it instead of letting it weigh me down. I had concealed this incident from everybody so far, but now I felt it was important to share it. With a deep breath, I said, 'After our project in Pune was completed, Rathore organised a visit to a famous Saibaba temple. I had been eager pay homage at the sacred site for a long time.'

Uttam leaned in with curiosity and interjected, 'Shirdi Waley Saibaba, Sir?'

'Yes,' I replied, acknowledging his familiarity with the pilgrimage destination. 'What made the trip truly memorable was that Aziz had accompanied me. He was a Muslim, and yet he didn't have to think twice before visiting a temple with me. We had walked through the temple together, and then we had prayed together. I recall it as a beautiful moment of religious harmony and acceptance.'

The room nodded appreciatively and Uttam remarked, '*Kya baat hai, Sir.*'

'Aziz's actions had manifested in his incredible broadmindedness. He was open-hearted, a quality I admired in him. I remember wishing the world had more people like him,' I continued.

'But did something change in just a day? Something terrible happened and Aziz was driven to commit a terrible act of violence? Three people have lost their lives and Aziz, too, is dead,' one employee asked, sounding very concerned.

'I don't know what happened, nor if or why he did what he did. But it breaks my heart to recall the man I once knew, and the tragic turn his life took,' I said, staring into the distance, my heart heavy with grief.

Sharing my story lifted a weight off my shoulders, but my sadness and regret did not dissipate. The room felt heavier, and the silence was deafening. Everybody slowly shuffled out of the office, with obviously heavy hearts and condolences on their lips. I was left alone with my thoughts, struggling to comprehend the futility of the last two days' events. My emotions were a strange combination of sorrow and anger. It was also like a part of me was divorced from my consciousness. I sat in the office, staring into thin air, lost in thought.

Time slipped away from me, darkness crept in, and Dori Lal returned to switch on the lights. Abruptly, I snapped out of my reverie. He coughed, holding my attention, and I turned to look at him.

I stood up from the sofa, noticing a stiffness in my legs. Dori Lal knew exactly what I needed: a chance to clear my head and refresh my senses. Wordlessly, he asked me to follow him and led me to the washroom. As I splashed water on my face, I felt detached from reality, as if everything around me was happening in a stereotypical, cinematic slow motion. Dori Lal walked in, offering me tea and suggesting I make a round of the exchange before he served me dinner. I looked up at him gratefully, sensing the genuineness of his concern for me.

'Thank you,' I said softly and, following his commands, sipped some of the much-needed hot tea and then started for the door of my office.

'I need some fresh air,' I told him.

He nodded in agreement. *'Ji saheb, aapko achcha lageyga.'*

I managed a gentle smile. Indeed, Dori Lal was right, I needed a reason to feel better.

~

As dusk fell and the night deepened, I resumed working, checking the paperwork, but my mind kept drifting to the loss of Aziz and the violent end he had met.

After dinner and the usual call home, Dori Lal set up my bed on the sofa. The winter chill had set in, and my office was no longer a warm and welcoming place. Cold air seeped in through every nook and cranny, making it impossible to sleep without a thick duvet wrapped around me. I couldn't begin comprehending how that army soldier stood on guard outside the gate in this weather.

As I settled in to sleep, I heard a familiar buzz: the sound of mosquitoes browsing for their next meal. Despite the cold, the pesky insects seemed to thrive, and I thanked Dori Lal silently for arranging a mosquito repellent. I extended my hand towards the switch by the side of the sofa and turned it on.

As I put myself back under the covers, I felt uneasy.

The darkness outside amplified my feeling of isolation. The chilly weather had penetrated my bones. I longed for the warmth of home, the comfort of a familiar place. But I knew I had to tough it out. I had work to do and couldn't let my feelings—like the weather or the mosquitoes—get in the way.

But try as I might, I couldn't shake the sadness lingering in my mind. Aziz's bearded face flashed before me the moment I closed my eyes, and a lump would form in my throat. His countenance repeatedly switched from saintly to cruel with unsettling frequency. His demeanour transitioned from pious to brutal in seconds. One moment, he wore a serene, almost beatific smile, and in the next moment, he revealed a twisted, crooked grin that could chill the soul. It was as if he had two distinct personalities at war, one pure and kind, the other dark and evil.

His appearance was a puzzle that begged for a solution, yet remained enigmatic and mysterious. In my mind, two scenes flashed relentlessly, one of him stabbing three men and the other capturing the tragic moment when the police ruthlessly shot him down. My mind also raced with thoughts of the family and loved ones of the three people Aziz had killed and the pain they must be feeling at this moment. I couldn't fathom the grief and shock that they must be going through. How could so many lives be taken so suddenly and without reason? My contradictory thoughts were maddening—I felt like I was being split into two people, one for Aziz and the other against him.

My pro-Aziz self told me that it is unfair to judge him without knowing all the facts. The possibility that Aziz was innocent lurked in a corner of my trusting heart. He could be a good man caught in a terrible situation. Maybe he was defending himself or others. But was my thinking along these lines trivialising the loss of three human lives? I asked myself this repeatedly in my dreamlike state.

The strict part of me reminded me that Aziz might always have harboured the capacity for violence, masquerading as a good person all along. Moreover, it seemed unjust that he had departed this world without facing the consequences of his actions. And the instant I entertained thoughts of his guilt, my sympathies for him would resurface, reminding me that amidst uncertainty, I had to be logical and not allow emotions to cloud my judgment.

Rationally, I felt I owed it to both Aziz and myself to find out the truth, no matter how unpalatable it was. If I could know the truth, I would certainly face it, and accept it. I cannot change the past, but I would learn from it and make better decisions in the future. The question is—how can one find out? Aziz and the three men were dead. The mob was gone. How would justice ever be delivered in this case?

Then, a voice rose within me: *If you just can't forget the feeling that you were wrong about him, how will you deal with his betrayal?*

Soon enough, I tilted towards the proverb that ignorance is bliss. What if, in seeking the truth, I discovered something I did not want to know? What if I just hadn't seen what Aziz was about? How would I deal with that? Consider all the possibilities, said my heart. It wanted me to do the impossible—ensure that justice is served, which my heart was aching for, including for the families of the victims.

All this time, the flashing images of the men being stabbed by Aziz countered my rational voice. Could I ever walk up to the families of these men and tell them that he was a good person who did something terrible? They have lost their loved ones because of him—could I justify that for any reason?

The voice continued: *You can't just ignore your thoughts about the families of the dead. Maybe they have lost their sole breadwinners.*

I wanted to reconcile these conflicting, arguing voices within me, for the chaos they were creating inside my head was getting too much to bear. Ultimately, I decided to acknowledge my limitations as a human being. I cannot know everything about everyone, and I can only do my best to understand those around me and trust them. When I feel betrayed, I can learn from it and strive to improve. But I cannot let guilt and betrayal consume me. I must focus on the truth and justice.

I understood the situation better then and decided that, given the chance, I would help the victims by ensuring justice through truth and accountability. I felt like I owed it to the families of the victims to do everything I could to find closure. Gradually, the conflict within me began to dissipate.

~

I was mentally and physically exhausted, but it was impossible to fall asleep. I tossed and turned, trying to push away the reminders of the bitter events of the day and focus on something else. Eventually, my thoughts drifted to work and the need to be strong for my team and carry on. Phone communications in the city of Bhopal depended on us like never before. After one last, deep sigh, I finally drifted off to sleep, hoping that tomorrow will be a better day.

Wrapped tight in the thick duvet to fend off the biting cold, I must have slept for two hours, which seemed to have lasted for a few minutes, when a high-pitched hum broke the quiet stillness of my office. The irritating mosquitoes were back. Roused from slumber, I sat up, and something started gnawing at me right away. It was not just the news of Aziz's death, though my subconscious had constantly been dwelling on it.

I realised that there was a power cut at the City Exchange, plunging us into complete darkness. That is why the repellent had stopped spewing its chemical soup, and the buzzing mosquitoes had swarmed around me. I felt their wings beating against my skin, and even the thick duvet was no match for their needle-like proboscises.

But something else was bothering me in the pitch-black night. Panic swelled within me, and my childhood fears resurfaced as I wondered if someone else was in the room with me, lurking in the shadows. My breathing filled my ears, and I heard my heart pounding in my chest. I fumbled for the landline phone, but found no dial tone.

Minutes ticked by as my fear grew stronger. I was alone in the dark with nothing to defend myself against the unknown. The dread of uncertainty began to consume me. Aziz's violent death amid the riots had intensified my terror. So, I thought, had anti-social elements deliberately cut off the power supply? Had danger finally found its way to my doorstep?

My duvet clung to me like a second skin. I threw it away, struggling to catch my breath. I stumbled towards the door, my heart loud in my chest, darkness enveloping me like a shroud, and I felt along the walls to avoid tripping over the furniture. As I fumbled for the doorknob, my hand brushed against something cold, and a shiver went down my spine. It was just the freezing knob, and with trembling hands, I turned and pushed the door open. It creaked eerily as if registering its protest for being disturbed.

The opened door revealed a dark corridor and a blast of cold wind cut through my clothes. I stood there, shivering in the stillness, wondering if I was the only one still alive in this godforsaken telephone exchange! Then, in the darkness of the corridor, I saw the faint glimmer of a distant light. I stepped out cautiously, walking into the unknown and towards the faint light.

It was then that I heard it—a high-pitched sound like an animal in pain. My heart pounded in my chest again as the sound grew louder, more intense, closer and closer. But I couldn't tell where it was coming from. Before I could recall that it was nothing but a squeaky door opening in the far end of the corridor, suddenly, glowing eyes appeared in the dark, staring at me. I froze with fear and panic.

Who was it? An animal? A human?

I could make out the figure of a person, his face appearing ghostly in the feeble flickering torchlight. He approached, and I was at a loss.

'Sir, is it you?' the figure asked in a voice that echoed through the empty corridor.

It was a moment before I recognised the voice. It was nonc other than AW Hassan, a special services operator at the City Exchange. He was one of four operators I had suspended from work some time back. The Special Services Exchange was also run from the City Exchange building.

'What are you doing out here?' I asked, shaking with fear.

The torchlight flickered and went out, plunging us in complete darkness. Hassan's hand gripped mine tight, and we stumbled blindly forward. Something wasn't right. The hair on the back of my neck stood on end, and I felt like someone was watching from the shadows.

The memory of that fateful day a month earlier, when I had suspended this man, flooded back. I had been forced to take action after uncovering evidence of serious misconduct at work. It was a difficult decision, but it was essential to preserve the integrity of our organisation. The echoes of the union's slogans against my decision resounded in my mind, as angry employees shouted and marched past the exchange building. I could hear their cries for justice, their demand to reinstate the suspended workers. The union leader was at the forefront, his voice hoarse from shouting. Each word felt like a threat, a warning of what could happen if I didn't comply with their demands. The tension in the air was palpable, and I remember wondering if I had made a mistake in suspending those employees.

The faces of those four suspended men, including Hassan's, flashed before me like scenes from a vivid dream in fast-forward motion.

रुक जाना नहीं तू कहीं हार के
काँटों पे चलके मिलेंगे साये बहार के
रुक जाना नहीं तू कहीं हार के
काँटों पे चलके मिलेंगे साये बहार के

Even in the depths of despair, don't linger or rest
Triumph awaits those who pass life's toughest tests.

CHAPTER FOUR

Sweet Dreams Turn Nightmares

AW Hassan's arrival that night was like a memory of the last wisp of a fading dream. On the day of the suspension, dinner with my family had been pleasant enough, yet a gnawing feeling clawed at me all evening, like an itch I couldn't scratch. I rationalised that I was upset because of the guilt of having broken the rules by using my official vehicle for personal reasons—going out for dinner with my family. Or, maybe the call of duty had stirred within me for no reason. At any rate, right after dinner, I felt compelled to act on a hunch.

As soon as we returned home as the clock struck midnight, I bid my family goodnight and then told my wife that I had decided to inspect the City Exchange. I offered no explanation, only the reassurance that I would return soon. I suddenly wanted to see whether the night duty staff were performing their duties diligently or slacking off.

The nighttime drive to the exchange was memorable. The darkness enveloped me like a cloak as I drove past the silent streets. My heart was pounding with a mix of apprehension and excitement, and I was unsure of what I would find when I arrived, but I had resolved to do my duty. I inserted a cassette into the player, hoping music would help calm my nerves. A famous melody started playing, filling the jeep with soothing notes.

रुक जाना नहीं तू कहीं हार के
काँटों पे चलके मिलेंगे साये बहार के

(In the depths of despair, don't linger or rest
Triumph awaits those who pass life's toughest tests.)

As I negotiated a right turn from the main road, I saw the City Exchange building. It loomed large and imposing, like a fortress guarding the secrets of the communication networks. Even when entering the exchange, the feeling that something was amiss stayed with me. I walked through the gloomy corridors with a sense of foreboding. The darkness felt like a physical weight on my chest. I was convinced something unexpected was about to occur.

I decided to inspect the Strowger Exchange first. It is a hive of activity during the day, but night is a different story, as only a few uni-selectors, group selectors, and final selectors are typically alive. The technicians there were diligently performing their duties. They were surprised to see me at that hour. One of them proudly informed me, 'Sir, we are doing preventive maintenance—to ensure faults do not occur during daytime.'

I patted their backs, and they responded with big smiles of acknowledgement and proceeded to the battery and power plants, followed by the generator and transformer rooms, and finally, the recently renovated trunk manual exchange. This exchange, now a monument to a bygone era of communication, then played a crucial role in connecting customers across cities. To initiate a trunk call, customers would dial the code '180', and the operator would respond, often groggily, requesting the desired destination number.

In those days, reaching out across distances required patience and perseverance. Customers would have to wait, depending on the priority of the booking—ordinary, urgent, or lightning—for their calls to be connected. Even then, their conversations were limited to merely three, six, or a maximum of nine minutes. Sometimes, an ordinary call meant a day-long wait for the customer, while urgent calls were connected to outstation numbers in hours, and lightning calls took minutes to connect.

Naturally, requests for urgent connections came at a steeper price tag. Charges would swell in accordance with the priority level, with lightning calls costing a hefty eight times as much as their ordinary counterparts. Additionally, by dialling the code '181', customers could assess any delay in their trunk booking or even cancel their calls, if required.

Such an arrangement for a phone call might sound prehistoric to today's youth, who have access to the internet and even video calls on their personal phones, but for the generation that has lived through the 1980s and 1990s, this was everyday life. In the past, bridging the physical gap with a simple phone call meant surmounting a logistical hurdle, not just a click of a personal phone. STD calls, a blessing in themselves, weren't even available to everybody. Booking a trunk call was like a ballet prearranged by skilled operators and crossed fingers, and it could mean enduring agonising delays while praying that the line wouldn't be a crackling mess of static.

Bridging distances once was like writing a love letter that a camel would deliver; definitely not for the faint-hearted. On the flip side, in the past, every conversation felt like a gemstone unearthed after a treasure hunt. Operators were treated like VIPs in the era of trunk-calling, and knowing one was a badge of social prestige. Many people would boast of such connections as symbols of their influence and access.

At the exchange, it was reassuring to see all employees working diligently, even without their senior officers. However, I was jolted out of my complacency on reaching the Special Service Section. This section catered to services such as directory enquiry '197', morning alarm facility '174', timekeeping service '173', and local number connection '199'. Invariably, there were complaints that these services did not function as they should at night and that the operators neglected subscribers.

That night, I witnessed the problem first-hand: the four special services operators on duty were in deep sleep on neatly laid mattresses adjacent to their office chairs. It infuriated me to see them lying there, shamelessly dressed for comfort in their vests and lungis. They had even locked the glass door of their office from inside. Seeing them sound asleep brought my anger to its boiling point. How could they display such carelessness and indifference towards their responsibilities? I pounded the door repeatedly, hoping they would awaken, but to no avail. For a second, I contemplated overlooking the situation and returning home. Why should I let their sleep disturb mine? However, soon, my frustration transformed into concern as I began to worry that they might be unconscious because of some medical emergency.

Impulsively, I rushed back to the trunk exchange and called the supervisor, asking him to come and look at the scene. The two of us then stood outside the door, banging relentlessly, when I noticed a sheepish expression on the supervisor's face. So he knew this time was not the first instance of these operators neglecting their duties. He had turned red with embarrassment, and I could see that he carried the weight of their neglect on his shoulders.

The supervisor turned to me with his eyes downcast. 'Sir, it's their daily routine,' he admitted. 'Most of them voluntarily ask for night duty and come here to sleep. Many times, they are intoxicated and, therefore, it becomes difficult to wake them up,' he said.

He paused before continuing, 'Sir, all four come from a suburban area called Bairagarh. They do other businesses during the day, so this job is almost secondary for them. They are also of the goon type and pick fights with anyone who tries to stop them.' His voice trailed off, and he looked at me with that same mix of guilt and resignation. Bairagarh was about six kilometres from the City Exchange and it had a predominantly Sindhi population.

I could see the trunk supervisor's helplessness and frustration at the situation. He knew that he had failed in his duty to ensure that his team was performing its tasks diligently. He knew he had let down the public, who relied on his team to provide essential services. But it was also clear that he felt remorse for his inability to prevent this from happening. I felt some sympathy for this supervisor, but the damage was done, and the public had suffered because of the operators' neglect. It was clear that something had to be done, but what? I knew that it wouldn't be easy to get rid of these operators, given their connections and influence.

Yet, I also knew that I couldn't let this circus continue. I had to find a way to hold them accountable and ensure that such negligence didn't recur. Inside the locked special services section, the big pilot lamp was turning on and switching off above the sleeping operators, indicating that customers were trying in vain to reach the exchange. The thought of people having missed an important call or failing to reach an emergency service because of their negligence filled me with rage. It was disappointing for me and for all the people affected by this, from students who needed to wake up early to study to those trying to catch an early morning train and those who desperately needed the number of a utility service or a hospital in an emergency.

I turned to the supervisor and requested him to record the incident in the logbook with his signature and present it to me officially the following day. He was momentarily reluctant, for he knew the severe consequences this would have for the operators. He also knew that these derelict operators could take revenge on him. However, I was single-minded about ensuring justice and convinced him to take action. The following day, in the morning, the logbook was brought to me, and with utmost care, I inscribed my note in striking red ink with the words:

'The undersigned, during a visit to the city telephone exchange at 0100 hours, observed the aforementioned special services operators sound asleep on duty. Consequently, exercising my disciplinary authority as the Divisional Engineer, I, Anupam Shrivastava, hereby suspend these operators effective immediately. Subsequently, individual charge sheets under Rule 14 shall be prepared, and requisite disciplinary measures shall be initiated in accordance with applicable provisions of the Post and Telegraph Rules.'

News of the suspension and issuance of charge sheets to the operators spread like wildfire, and my phone began ringing incessantly. I received two types of calls: from those who applauded my decision to take action against the negligent operators and others from individuals attempting to intimidate me by highlighting the potential consequences of my decision.

Amidst the uproar, NP Lalwani, a union leader, paid me a visit with two of his colleagues. He was quick to demand the withdrawal of my order, citing the ongoing national secretary general election contest between OP Gupta and Namboodiri.

'Sir, this is not the right time to take such action. Employees from all over the country have assembled in Bhopal for the union's national general secretary election, and your decision could impact the process. If you want to take action, please wait a fortnight,' he said, curtailing the antagonism inherent in his words by making them sound like an advisory.

I listened intently, but I had already decided and couldn't back down now. I replied, 'Mr Lalwani, I appreciate your concern, but it's too late. I have already taken disciplinary action. Reversing my decision would send the wrong signal and could lead to further indiscipline. I cannot afford that.'

From my chair, I watched Lalwani exit, his contempt evident in his gait. Suddenly, Hassan, the suspended operator, approached me. His presence felt suffocating. He slammed his palm on my desk. 'Listen closely,' he snarled, with his eyes piercing through me. 'Antagonising our union carries dire repercussions. You've been warned. Remember, retract your action, or we have ways to make you disappear from your position.'

Quickly, Lalwani turned around, looking at me sternly. However, he composed himself swiftly and took charge of the situation. He apologised and advised his colleague to control himself and not speak rudely to me, '*Hassan miyan, apney aap par control rakho, saheb ke saamney aise nahi boltay.*'

'I'm sorry about him, Sir. Hassan is just a little emotional right now. Please don't take it personally. However, I still urge you to consider our request or else be prepared to face the consequences,' he quickly added, looking at me and not mincing his words.

I crossed my arms and fixed a stern gaze on them, simultaneously tapping the floor as a signal of disagreement and annoyance. However, deep within, I had a lingering sense of danger ahead. The situation had grown more complex than I anticipated, and I realised the need for caution. The election for the national general secretary hung in the balance, and I couldn't afford to let my actions jeopardise the outcome. Yet, I couldn't ignore the operators' negligence towards their duties. It was a delicate balancing act, requiring me to make a thoughtful decision.

Within the next hour, the rival group of union workers led by Uttam Sharma also visited me. He approached me with a smile and said, 'Sir, we congratulate you on your bold action. This will help improve services and workers' efficiency.' His supporters suddenly started raising slogans in my praise. 'Anupam Shrivastava, Zindabad! Zindabad! DE Saheb, Zindabad! Zindabad!'

The unwanted attention was getting to me. I always loved to work silently and was shy of public attention. 'Thank you, Uttam,' I replied. 'But I only did what was necessary to maintain discipline and ensure our services are unaffected.'

Uttam smiled again and said, 'Yes, Sir, we know. But you took a brave step and showed that you are committed to improving our services. We appreciate your efforts.' He said, 'We haven't seen any officer come to inspect the exchange at 1:00 a.m.–1:30 a.m. in at least the last twenty-five years.'

I thanked him again but still felt uncomfortable. I knew this event could heighten inter-union rivalry, with one supporting and the other opposing my decision. That evening, after office hours, I stepped out of the exchange building and found myself swarmed by journalists from Hindi and English newspapers. They sought my reasons for the incident of the previous night. I drew in a deep breath, attempting to compose myself before speaking. I recounted the details of what had happened, explaining how I had uncovered the negligence of the four operators and the disciplinary measures I had taken against them.

'Mr Shrivastava, can you tell us more about the disciplinary action you have taken?' one of the journalists enquired.

I replied, 'Yes, I suspended the operators immediately, pending a thorough investigation. Their actions were unacceptable.'

Another journalist asked, 'What is your opinion on the state of telephone services in Bhopal?'

I answered cautiously, 'I believe there is always room for improvement. It is essential for all of us to prioritise customer satisfaction.'

'I would also like to commend the role of both unions in helping to address the issue. We must work together to ensure that our services meet the highest standards for the people of Bhopal. This incident has emphasised the need for continued collaboration and communication among all involved parties,' I added.

The journalists nodded approvingly, and one asked, 'Do you anticipate any changes in how telephone services are conducted following this incident?'

'I sincerely hope so,' I replied. 'It is critical that we hold ourselves and each other accountable for the quality of our services.'

I noticed the journalists were nodding in agreement and eagerly jotting notes. They probed me for more information about my background, experience, and views on the conditions of telephone services in Bhopal.

Despite the intrusive journalistic scrutiny, I remained poised and provided honest responses. I understood that this was an opportunity to shed light on an important issue and to raise awareness about accountability and responsibility. After an eternity, the journalists prepared to depart. I wondered who had summoned them and how their stories would be reported in the news the following day.

On arriving home, I noticed my wife and father's worried expressions. They told me that they had been receiving threatening calls on our landline. The callers had been using vulgar language and threatening to make me revoke the disciplinary action. Just then, the phone rang, and I picked it up.

'Hello?' I said.

'You think you're so smart, suspending us?' said the sneering voice on the other end.

It was one of the suspended operators.

'I had to take disciplinary action,' I replied calmly. 'Your negligence caused our customers problems, and that is unacceptable.'

'We don't give a damn about the customers,' the suspended operator spat out his words. 'We're tired of you treating us like dirt. You had better take back your action, or you'll regret it,' he said.

'I can't do that,' I said firmly. 'My responsibility is to maintain the quality of our services.'

'You'll regret this,' the operator growled before hanging up.

It didn't take long before he called again.

Trying to remain calm, I answered. The suspended operator hurled insults and threats at me.

'You have no right to treat us this way!' he shouted. 'We have families and social prestige, but everyone is laughing at us because of you. You'll regret what you have done!'

I tried to reason with him. He only laughed bitterly at me.

'Customers?' he repeated, mocking me. 'Do you think you care about the customers? All you care about is your power and authority. Well, you're going to regret crossing our path. We'll make you pay for this,' he said. I heard the anger and resentment in his voice and knew that this was not a situation I could handle alone. I ended the call and immediately called the police, explaining the situation and requesting their assistance.

As I hung up the phone, my wife and father looked at me with concern. 'What's going on?' my wife asked.

'It's the suspended operators,' I explained. 'I called the police about their threats, but we need to be careful.'

My father nodded grimly. 'We'll do what it takes to protect our family,' he said. It was a difficult situation, but I had to see it through. I kept receiving calls late into the night until I took the receiver off the cradle. Finally, there was peace and quiet in my home.

The next day, in my office, two newspapers were on my table. I shuffled through the pages and noted the news items covering the last few days' events.

In English, one of the news reports said:

'Sweet Dreams Turn Nightmarish'

Free Press News Service

BHOPAL, Oct 11

The telecom employees, who were supposed to man the essential services in the City Exchange, were literally jolted out of their sweet dreams, and found themselves facing the hard reality of a charge sheet, presented to them by the Divisional Engineer of the City Exchange, Anupam Shrivastava, at 1:30 a.m. last night.

Shrivastava made a surprise visit to the exchange last night and found, to his horror, all the employees deputed to man the essential services like '197', '199', '185', and '181' blissfully asleep, while the receivers were off the hooks, so that no one could disturb their sweet dreams.

Shrivastava took prompt action and charged all the erring employees on the spot, who had converted the office into a dormitory.

A pleasant aspect of the whole affair has been the support given by both the employee unions to the action taken against the employees.

Normally, employees' unions oppose any administrative action taken against the employees, but in this instance, they did not have any moral ground to oppose the action, the office bearers of the unions said.

That Shrivastava's action had been effective was proved today when one got a reply from the above-mentioned services right after the first ring, while previously, one either got the engaged tone continuously or there seemed to be no one present to man the services and one generally hung up after the innumerable rings went unanswered.

Another effect of the action was that now, while answering the services, the voice very courteously says "Sir" in response to a query. Earlier it was a voice which sounded almost abusive. Thanks a ton, Shrivastava.'

And this is how the Hindi newspapers reported it:

वे ड्यूटी पर लुंगी लपेटे सो रहे थे
नगर प्रतिनिधि, भोपाल।

लोगो की शिकायतों की आकस्मिक जांच की एक योजना के अनुसार सिटी एक्सचेंज के विभागीय डिविज़नल इंजीनियर श्री अनुपम श्रीवास्तव ने गत दिन जब रात्रि डेढ़ बजे एक्सचेंज का निरीक्षण किया तो वे यह देख कर हैरान रह गये कि टेलीफोन के अत्यावश्यक सेवाओं वाले नंबरों पर तैनात कर्मचारी बाकायदा बिस्तर लगा कर लुंगी पहन कर सो रहे थे। रिसीवर हुकों पर लटके थे जिससे किसी भी टेलीफोन करने वाले उपभोक्ता को लगातार एंगेज टोन ही मिले। १६७, १६६, १८० और १८१ नम्बरों पर तैनात कर्मचारी बाकायदा खर्राटे ले रहे थे।

श्री श्रीवास्तव ने रात में ही प्रशासनिक कार्यवाही की और कार्यालय को शयन कक्ष में तब्दील करने वाले इन कर्मचारियों को तुरंत चार्ज शीट थमा दी। श्री अनुपम श्रीवास्तव की इस कार्यवाही से सारे कार्यालय में खलबली मच गई। इस प्रकरण का एक सुखद पहलू यह भी सामने आया कि कर्मचारियों के दोनों संगठनों ने कर्तव्य के प्रति इस कदर लापरवाही बरतने वाले कर्मचारियों के खिलाफ कार्यवाही का समर्थन किया है। सामान्यतः संगठन कर्मचारियों के खिलाफ किसी भी प्रशासनिक कार्यवाही पर ऐतराज उठाते हैं लेकिन उनका कहना है कि इस तरह के मामलों में जहां कर्तव्य का इतना दुर्लक्ष्य हो रहा हो वे, कोई औचित्यपूर्ण विरोध नहीं कर सकते।

श्री श्रीवास्तव के इस निरीक्षण का एक तत्काल प्रभाव यह हुआ है, कि आवश्यक सेवाओं पर तैनात कर्मचारी पहले से अधिक चौकन्ने हो गये है और दूरभाष की इन सेवाओं में सुधार भी परिलक्षित हुआ है।

I was basking in the joy of the news reports when the jarring sound of my landline phone abruptly stopped my thoughts in their tracks. I wavered for a fleeting moment, a hint of anxiety gripping me as I contemplated answering the call. I feared it would be the same men who had been abusing me all night. Regrettably, my apprehensions were confirmed as I recognised the malevolent voice of one of the operators. Involuntarily, my heart sank, and I steeled myself for another onslaught of insults and threats.

'Don't think you've escaped,' he snarled in a venomous tone. 'We'll ensure you rue the day you made that decision.'

'You are pushing the boundaries too far,' I exclaimed, my voice rising as I drew confidence from the positive coverage of my decision by the newspapers. 'Have you not checked today's newspapers?' I added, emphasising the significance of the published information.

'You orchestrated the unfavourable news coverage about us through your connections in the media,' the man accused with a tone of certainty.

Before I could respond, the line abruptly went dead. An unsettling combination of concern and fear gripped my thoughts. Just then, a cacophony of slogans pierced the air, drawing my attention to the window. I looked out and witnessed a gathering of employees, led by the authoritative figure of Lalwani, brandishing banners and united in their uproar. Lalwani led the crowd in chanting 'Anupam Shrivastava...*haaye, haaye*', to which the crowd responded with a chorus of '*haaye, haaye!*'

He continued, 'DE internal...haaye, haaye,' and the crowd responded in unison again.

'*Jo humsay takrayega...*' he declared, and the crowd responded, '...*Choor-choor ho jayega!*' (Those who challenge us will be crushed.)

He added, '*Humari mangey poori karo...*', and the crowd responded,' '*Operators ko wapis lo, bahal karo!*' (Fulfil our demands, and reinstate the operators.)

At the end, Lalwani proclaimed, 'Suspended operators *ko bahal karo,*' and the crowd responded with determination, '*Bahal karo, bahal karo!*'

Immediately, I called my boss, Gokul Singh, and briefed him on the situation.

'You'll be able to manage it,' he said confidently. 'Just stay calm and resolute.' He hung up, leaving me to contemplate his words.

I then called CGM Gupta. He advised me: 'Anupam, this is your opportunity to learn an important lesson for your career. You must learn to manage such situations if you want to succeed.' Then he, too, hung up, and I wondered at the faith my bosses had in me.

Feeling encouraged, I turned my attention back to the window and saw Lalwani approaching my office.

'Mr Lalwani, what brings you here?' I asked, trying to maintain a calm demeanour.

'We're here to negotiate a deal,' he replied. 'We're willing to come to an agreement, but you must meet our demands.'

As we discussed the terms, I wondered whether I could handle this high-pressure situation. Although Lalwani's words were polite and seemed sincere, I was alert and suspicious. He apologised for the earlier disturbance, but I suspected that he was playing some sort of game.

'I can understand what you are trying to say,' I replied, striving to maintain composure in my voice. 'However, the conduct of our special services operators was utterly unacceptable. Their actions not only disrupted operations but also set a deplorable precedent, tarnishing the reputation of our organisation.'

Lalwani nodded empathetically, his voice lowering to a hushed tone. 'I wholeheartedly concur with your sentiments, Sir. Rest assured; we have taken decisive measures to ensure that such an incident is never repeated. We have already initiated stringent action against these operators and barred them from participating in union activities in the future.'

With a raised eyebrow and a hint of sarcasm, I expressed disbelief and winked in astonishment. 'Oh, really? That's just fantastic, so what were those charming slogans you were shouting just now?'

Lalwani leaned back, his expression turning very serious, and said, 'That was just union posturing, Sir. You know it quite well. We wanted to bring the issue to your attention in front of our members. But we are willing to negotiate a solution that works for everyone.'

Eager to strike a deal, he went on, 'Sir, I want to

personally convey to you how much I respect you as an administrator. I have always supported your strict actions to improve services. You are doing a great job, and I acknowledge that. I also understand that some operators' behaviour has been a concern, and we will take strict action against these members of our union.'

I heard sincerity in Lalwani's words and realised that he was not just making a political move. It seems he genuinely appreciated my working style and I could believe his promise of action against those responsible. I decided to see if we could find a mutually acceptable solution.

'I appreciate your offer, Mr Lalwani,' I said, keeping my tone neutral. 'But I'm not sure if that's possible. These operators have shown a clear lack of professionalism and put the entire department's reputation at stake. I cannot overlook their misconduct.'

'I understand, but I assure you that we will ensure that they behave impeccably for the next two weeks. Once the election is over, we will not interfere in your decisions regarding their punishment,' Lalwani said.

After a moment of silence, I replied, 'Okay, Mr Lalwani. I will agree to your request and reinstate these operators for a fortnight. But I want to be clear. If they repeat any misbehaviour, they will be terminated immediately. Please ask all four operators to write a letter to me apologising for their actions and pleading reinstatement.'

Lalwani smiled gratefully, 'Thank you, Sir. I will

tell them to write immediately. I assure you again that you will not regret this decision.'

I nodded, relieved that the situation had been resolved for now. But the uncertainty about what might happen once the union election was over remained. Only time would tell.

To our astonishment, the four operators obstinately refused to respond to the suspension letter or plead for reinstatement. They expected me to unconditionally retract the suspension letter. Consequently, the union eventually ceased its pursuit of the case. And, in those days before phone calls could be easily tracked or traced back to their source, I found myself persistently plagued by menacing calls at the most unexpected hours.

नफ़रत जो सिखाये वो धरम तेरा नहीं है
इन्सां को जो रौंदे वो कदम तेरा नहीं है
कुरआन न हो जिसमे वो मंदिर नहीं तेरा
गीता न हो जिसमे वो हरम तेरा नहीं है

The religion that teaches hatred is not yours
No step that tramples humans is yours
No temple is yours where there is no Quran
The Kaaba is not yours if it has no Gita.

CHAPTER FIVE

Midnight

December 8

I was being dragged towards the 12x10 storeroom attached to the dark corridor of the City Exchange building. My mind grappled unsuccessfully with fear and uncertainty. I could feel the sweat trickling down my forehead despite the cold winter night as I imagined the worst. Was Hassan seeking revenge for the disciplinary action I took against him? Or did he plan to harm me in the garb of the ongoing riots?

As we entered the dark storeroom, I instinctively searched for an escape route but could see none. Hassan remained silent; staring at me with an eerie intensity.

'What's going on?' I asked at last, trembling with panic.

He answered, almost in a whisper, 'Sir, I'm not here to harm you.'

As I blinked in surprise, he explained, 'The telephone

exchange is under attack from rioters. Three members of the mob had approached me with a scheme to sabotage the exchange tonight. They wanted me to accompany them as they felt that I would have a score to settle with you after my suspension.'

Then, he subtly indicated that I take the chair behind a nearby table, and I gently pulled the chair towards me and sat down, trying to process the meaning of his words. Was it some kind of trick? Did he have a hidden agenda?

'I was with them, but, as you know, I've been earning my livelihood from this organisation,' he continued, leaning against the table that separated us.

'Three of my associates have disrupted the electricity supply, which is why the power is out. They have somehow torn the fuse of the CTPT,' he said.

'Oh, my God,' I exclaimed.

He was referring to the transformer, technically known as the Current Transformer Potential Transformer, through which the 11 KV power supply to the exchange is routed. Unless the fuse was replaced, the exchange would soon stop operating. And this transformer was placed on a pole located outside the boundary wall of the exchange, which made the repair work complicated in the current situation.

In a daze, my eyes moved to take in the view beyond the single window in the storeroom. Outside, the soft glow of moonlight enveloped the exchange.

Then Hassan's voice, still barely above a whisper,

brought me back into the room. His body tensed slightly as he eyed the door, vigilant for any sound of movement. 'I knew that you have been living inside the exchange for two days,' he confided, his words hushed and urgent, 'I separated myself from the others in the mob as soon as I could and hastened to warn you.'

I closed my eyes briefly, allowing his words to sink in. When I opened them to look at him, I expected him to say more.

With utmost sincerity, he pleaded, 'I implore you to summon the army personnel stationed at the gate without delay. These individuals causing trouble are not hardened criminals; they are merely agitated due to the recent events in Ayodhya. Once confronted, they will quickly retreat. It is crucial that we act swiftly to protect our telephone exchange.'

His words resonated with truth, and pierced the stress that hung heavily in the storeroom. Without a moment's hesitation, we moved swiftly and silently towards the main gate. Hassan trailed me like a shadow. At the gate, I wasted no time in alerting the army personnel stationed there. The urgency in my voice mirrored the exigency of our situation and the soldiers, trained and disciplined, promptly assembled, their eyes reflecting steely determination.

When they stood before me, they looked formidable, a force capable of defending the telephone exchange and its people. Clad in protective gear and armed with weapons, they exuded a confidence that bolstered my resolve.

Suddenly, a single gunshot shattered the silence, reverberating through the night. The sound seemed to echo for miles. The saboteurs, who had been inching closer to the Trunk Exchange, were caught off guard, their sinister plans to disrupt the communication services were disrupted.

The soldiers sprang into action, their training taking over. Another shot rang out, a warning to the perpetrators, a signal that their malicious intent would not go unchallenged. It created a commotion that filled the air, a testament to the determination of those protecting the exchange.

Faced with this unexpected resistance, the saboteurs faltered. Fear crept into their hearts, urging them to abandon their destructive mission. Like shadows fleeing from light, they hastily changed course, desperately seeking an escape route. Their figures, illuminated by the moonlight, appeared as fleeting silhouettes against the night sky. One of the army personnel aimed at the fleeting silhouettes and, through the corner of his eyes, sought affirmation to shoot. I tilted my head back, raised my chin, and shook my head, prompting the soldier to lower his aim. The three intruders, distinct in their desperation, frantically scaled the walls of the exchange and hastily raced away. They disappeared into the night, and then the sound of their footsteps faded away.

We watched their retreat, knowing that we had successfully thwarted a sinister plan. The telephone exchange stood strong, safeguarded by the bravery of the soldiers. As the adrenaline rush subsided, a sense of gratitude engulfed us. Gratitude for the swift response of the army personnel, and for the unity and resilience that had prevailed in adversity.

We stood there in the still night, the gibbous moon casting a gentle glow upon us, allowing ourselves a moment to absorb the significance of what had just transpired. The threat had been averted, but the need for vigilance remained; it was a reminder of the fragility and importance of the connections we often take for granted.

With a renewed sense of purpose, we turned our attention back to the telephone exchange, knowing that our duty to protect it was far from over. The night was not yet over. Hassan and I walked towards the engine room. He turned to me and said, 'Sir, I am aware of my mistakes, but I couldn't stand by as our workplace was destroyed. I am sorry for my past actions, and hope you will forgive me.'

I observed a man who had been granted a second chance and had consciously opted to do what was right despite his past wrongdoings. In that tender instant, I realised that the realm of possibilities expanded infinitely when we had a shared purpose. A deep sense of appreciation welled up within me for Hassan. In an intense and perilous situation, thanks to his timely alert, we had averted a catastrophe. In that moment, the dichotomy of boss and employee dissolved, leaving just two individuals united by a common objective—to safeguard the telephone exchange and ensure that the phone lines kept working despite the social unrest.

I placed my hand gently on his shoulder, and saw tears began to form in Hassan's eyes. I would have offered him some words of comfort but my focus was abruptly captured by the hushed stillness of the engine plant. The silence meant that power supply had been severed, and the exchange was reliant only on its dwindling battery reserves. Panic swept through me as realisation dawned: the Strowger Exchange battery was already teetering on the brink, with just enough energy to sustain operations for a mere hour. My heart sank, gripped by the notion that the battery was already depleted—it was why the telephone next to my bed was silent when I had lifted the receiver a short while ago.

I glanced at Hassan, and he had divined my thoughts. With a swift gesture to wipe away his tears, he spoke up, 'Sir, when I entered the exchange sometime back with the rioters, I heard a technician say that if the power supply was disrupted for more than an hour, the Strowger Exchange would stop working. This is because the stored diesel was used up during this evening's power outage, and because of the curfew, it was impossible to get more diesel.'

I frantically searched for a solution. The batteries of the E-10B and trunk exchanges were new, and could carry the load for ten hours without electricity supply. But the Strowger Exchange was a different story altogether. It was an old system, and the battery had seen better days. I closed my eyes, trying to remain calm in this predicament. I refused to let the telephone exchange succumb to the prevailing crisis, especially considering its significance in serving the riot-affected regions, where the rumour mill would take over if the existing communication lines went down.

There had to be a way out, a solution hidden in the recesses of my mind. I rushed to the battery room, my pulse racing with every step. As I arrived, I saw the anxious technicians. 'What's going on?' I asked.

One of the technicians turned to me and said, 'Sir, the engines are not running. We don't know what has gone wrong. The Strowger Exchange battery is depleted, and we can't recharge it without electricity.'

'The batteries of the E-10B and trunk exchange are new,' I said, my voice growing stronger with every word. 'Use them to power the Strowger Exchange.'

The operators looked at me, surprised at first and then hopefully. We rushed to the other battery room, and then, with the help of a thick, red wire, we connected the E-10B exchange battery to the Strowger Exchange battery. Within seconds, the exchange came back to life, and the dial tone was restored.

It was an interim solution, but a sigh of relief escaped me and the technicians' smiles mirrored my relief. *Small triumphs pave the path to greatness*, a resolute voice suddenly whispered within me. *Celebrate these small triumphs*, urged the inner voice. For a fleeting moment, an overwhelming surge of joy even tempted me to break into a dance, yet I resisted.

Then, one of the technicians spoke up. 'Sir, the power problem has only been deferred,' he said, breaking my momentary surge of happiness. 'With the current load at the Strowger Exchange, the batteries will last for approximately seven hours,' another technician informed.

'Which means we will run out by 9 or 9:30 a.m.,' he added.

As I roughly calculated the remaining time, I muttered under my breath, 'That leaves us with two options: either we acquire diesel before 9 a.m., or the 11 KV power supply needs to be restored by then.' If not, not only the Strowger Exchange, but every other machine in the exchange building will also no longer work.

I questioned myself—was connecting the Strowger exchange to the battery plant of the E-10B and Tax the right decision? Perhaps it was influenced by emotion, as I held direct responsibility for the functioning of that exchange and couldn't bear the thought of it not being operational.

We found ourselves in a dire situation; all the diesel shops nearby were closed due to the rioting and curfew, leaving us without a source of diesel for our engines. Our only viable option was to contact the Lineman from the state electricity board to repair the 11 KV supply. But we had to act right away. However, we faced an obstacle: we didn't have the contact number for the Madhya Pradesh Electricity Board substation. Typically, this information would be with the technician on duty at the transformer, but unfortunately, he had been unable to come for the night shift.

'I will drive to the nearest substation at Ret Ghat Chauraha next to the Alamgir mosque at Bada Talab,' I declared with unwavering resolve. 'I will bring the Lineman with me to repair the transformer's fuse,' I added firmly. However, the prospect of navigating the deserted streets in the curfew zone at 2:30 in the morning filled me with dread. I turned to the technicians and saw the worry reflected in their eyes.

'That's a risky move,' one said. 'Driving alone through these empty streets could be dangerous.'

'I can't let you go alone, Sir,' Prakash Ramani, one of the technicians, chimed in firmly, 'I'll come with you.'

Hassan, who had just turned from villain to hero, spoke up as well. 'I'll come, too,' he said.

I was grateful for their willingness to accompany me. We quickly made our way to my jeep parked in the porch of the exchange building and set off for the substation, navigating the darkened streets with caution. Lalwani and Hassan squeezed themselves on the front seat with me. The tension in the jeep was palpable, as we silently hoped and prayed that we reached our destination without incident.

Lalwani spoke up first. 'The situation is getting

worse, look at those burnt cars and scooters,' he said, pointing to wreckage lying on the sides of the road.

Hassan agreed, his voice equally tense. 'I heard on the news that there were clashes between Hindus and Muslims in this area. We should be careful,' he said, looking out of the window at deserted buildings and burnt shops. He tried to read their half-burnt boards. One read, 'Ahmad cycle repair' and the other, 'Rajesh Kirana store'.

I nodded grimly, my hands gripping the steering wheel tight and my eyes fixed on the road ahead. I noticed that Lalwani and Hassan had gripped the support rod in front of the jeep tightly. The headlights illuminated the eerily silent night streets. The air was thick with fear and uncertainty, and every turn seemed to bring us closer to danger. 'Just keep your eyes open and stay alert,' I said, sounding calm and firm, 'we'll get through this.'

As we drove further into the mess, we could hear the sounds of distant gunfire and shouting. It was almost suffocating, but we had a job to do, and would not let anything stand in our way. Pressing on, navigating the streets and dodging the debris along the way, was a nerve-wracking experience, but we finally arrived at our destination, the state electricity board's substation.

The substation building loomed before us imposingly, its entrance firmly closed. We disembarked and gathered in front of the massive gate. The surrounding emptiness engulfed us, and only a faint glimmer of light was visible from within the substation. We could hear the distant sound of waves crashing against the shores of Bhopal's famed Bada Talab lake. All of it created an eerie ambiance for an already unsettling night. To top it all, the almost full moon had begun its descent towards the horizon, casting long shadows of buildings and trees everywhere.

Lalwani approached me with urgency. 'Sir, about 500 metres away is the Budhwara locality, whose local MLA, Arif Aqueel, has allegedly incited the Muslim youth and distributed weapons, urging them to attack Hindus,' he revealed in a tone filled with concern and barely above whisper.

However, Hassan, who had overheard the remark, interjected with fervour, 'It's false! On the contrary, I saw him standing in front of a crowd of Muslims, preventing them from demolishing a temple. But nobody seems to believe us anymore. Aqueel Bhai has been arrested and put behind bars,' he said, sounding frustrated.

Like in the rest of the city of Bhopal, conflicting narratives and differing perspectives hung between us, too. I needed to shift focus, so I took charge and asserted, 'Let us set aside these disputes for now. Our priority is to establish a connection with the electricity board staff.' So, we simply shouted for attention at the gates, making our echoes reverberate through the empty space. Within a moment, a lineman emerged from behind the firmly shut door.

The Lineman on duty did not step outside the protective field of the collapsible gate as I explained the situation to him. 'I am a Divisional Engineer from the City Exchange. We need a repair team to fix the transformer's fuse at the City Telephone Exchange,' I said.

The Lineman's face was grave as he listened. 'Sir, I could have called the repair party from Bairagarh to your exchange,' he said. 'But our telephone went dead sometime back.'

I knew that this could be because the Strowger Exchange had run out of power, but since it was back in action, the line should be working again. When the duty Lineman checked this on my instruction, he found the telephone back in action. He dialled the substation in Bairagarh and requested them to reach the City Exchange quickly.

'We need to get there as soon as possible,' I said to my colleagues, 'Let's hope the repair team arrives quickly.'

We drove back through the same streets. The army personnel were standing smartly at the main gate and saluted us. There were no lights in the building as the exchanges were working on battery power. I decided to go inside the Strowger Exchange since it had a few emergency lights. It was already 3:30 in the morning, but I decided to call Col Ramanujam. To my surprise, he answered the call on the first ring and quickly recognised my voice.

'Hello, Colonel,' I began. 'Sorry to...'

Before I could finish my sentence, he warmly interjected, 'Hello, Mr Shrivastava. I know you've been on duty at the exchange for two days, day in and day out. Just half an hour ago, my men stationed at the exchange informed me about the attempted sabotage and how bravely you handled it.'

'Thank you, Colonel, but the credit truly belongs to your men,' I replied, gratefully. 'If not for them, phone lines in Bhopal would have been on the verge of collapse tonight. The situation is still dire as we don't have diesel to power the engines. Some intruders burnt the 11 KV transformer fuse, leading to a blackout at the exchange,' I explained, stumbling under the weight of stress and fatigue.

'You should have told me earlier,' he said, adding, 'we have a huge stock of diesel. I will send it to you between 10 and 10:30 tomorrow morning.'

Seeing hope glimmer again, I quickly added, 'Thank you, Colonel, but that would be too late. Our batteries can only handle the load of the exchange until 9-9:30 a.m.'

'In that case,' he said, 'I will immediately have the warehouse opened and send you a barrel of diesel as fast as possible.'

The next two hours involved waiting anxiously for a resolution to our problem. I made several rounds of the battery plant, checking the readings to see how much power was left and trying to calculate how long it would last. Around 7 a.m., a team from the electricity board arrived and immediately went to the corner of the exchange where, on two strong poles, the transformer was installed. Within an hour, they announced that the fuse had been fixed and requested our telephone exchange technicians to flip the circuit breaker on. The power came on momentarily, but the transformer fuse blew itself out again with a huge bang. The team rushed back to the pole to look for the fault.

The exchange would discharge within an hour. It was 8:30 a.m., and we paced back and forth. I sat in the battery plant, inhaling the acid fumes and praying. Just then, a technician came running and informed us that diesel sent by the army had arrived. We were ecstatic, as it was the best news we had received in a while. Everyone rushed towards the engine room, and the barrel of diesel was emptied into the engine. It was 9 a.m., only a few minutes before the batteries discharged, making all exchanges to collapse and cutting off communication in the city of Bhopal.

If that happened, even if power was restored, it would take three to four hours before the E-10B and Tax exchanges could be rebooted. It was 9:15 a.m. by the time the diesel was refilled, and now it was time to switch on the engine. The technician, his hand shaking with anxiety, pressed the start button. The 200 KV engine coughed to life with a deep rumble. It made a strange sound at first, but then it started whirring steadily. The engine showed that it was generating

230 Volts. The technician quickly flipped a switch, and the exchange power load shifted to the engine. The engine's crescendo rose to a strained whine at the sudden surge in demand. We held our breath, hoping the engine withstood the load. The readings on the voltmeter stabilised and the readings on the Ammeter gradually rose from zero to 75 amperes. The engine was running, making deep and robust sounds. It was like singing a low-pitch metallic song, punctuated by brief, high-pitch whines.

At 9:30 a.m., the engines were efficiently shouldering the load and recharging the batteries. The metres were flickering, and the hum of the engine was music to our ears. At that moment, the transformer fuse was also fixed, and the electricity supply returned. With every reason to smile, I strolled back to my office.

अल्लाह तेरो नाम, ईश्वर तेरो नाम
अल्लाह तेरो नाम, ईश्वर तेरो नाम
सबको सन्मति दे भगवान
सबको सन्मति दे भगवान

Allah is your name, and Ishwar, too
Grant everyone blessings, O divine flame.

CHAPTER SIX

A Change of Heart

December 9

On returning to my room, I looked in the mirror, noticing how my stubble had grown over the past three days. My eyes were bloodshot due to sleep deprivation. I had donned the appearance of a different person. After splashing water on my face and tidying my hair, I returned to my office and settled back in my chair. The room had been cleaned; the pillow and duvet removed from the sofa and taken away. The peon had switched on a built-in transistor on my tabletop watch, which was playing a song on the Vivid Bharati channel—

अल्लाह तेरो नाम
ईश्वर तेरो नाम

(Allah is your name
And Ishwar, too.)

I glanced at the calendar in front of me, seeing that it was Wednesday, December 9, 1992. I had been at the city telephone exchange for 48 hours at a stretch.

Meanwhile, the first stanza of the song played on the transistor-watch:

> माँगों का सिन्दूर ना छूटे
> माँगों का सिन्दूर ना छूटे
> माँ बहनो की आस ना टूटे
> माँ बहनो की आस ना टूटे
>
> (Let women not become widows
> Let women not become widows
> Let the hopes of mothers
> And sisters remain intact.)

The song came to an abrupt halt as the radio announcer's voice cut in, saying it was time for the news. The poignant lyrics had stirred me up, and my thoughts drifted towards the countless women who had been widowed, as well as the mothers and sisters who had lost the breadwinners of their households, leaving them with shattered dreams and uncertain futures. For a fleeting second, my thoughts again turned to Aziz. In a sense, that man had become a metaphor for everything uncanny about the situation.

Just then, with sharp beeps preceding, the news bulletin broke the silence in the room. The news broadcast commenced precisely at 11 a.m., and it had the latest updates on the ongoing riots in Bhopal:

'This is All India Radio.

The news, read by Rabia Bano.

The city of Bhopal continues to be tense following violent clashes between two communities. Curfew has been clamped for an indefinite period in old Bhopal with the army and paramilitary forces deployed to maintain law and order.

The situation remains volatile, with incidents of arson and violence being reported from these parts of the city despite shoot-at-sight orders. Dusk to dawn curfew from 6 p.m. to 6 a.m. has been clamped in New Bhopal. The situation in new Bhopal, however, is said to be under control.

In the latest development, the Bhopal Collector Shri MA Khan and SP Shri Subhash Atre have been replaced by Shri Pravesh Sharma and Shri Surendra Singh respectively. The move is seen as an attempt to bring in fresh leadership to control the situation and restore normalcy.

As a precautionary measure under Section 151 of the Criminal Procedure Code, the state government decided to arrest Shri Arif Aqueel, MLA, in Bhopal. Shri Lokendra Singh, former MP of the BJP, in Panna, Shri Ramanand Singh, MLA of Janata Dal, and Shri Yogendra Rana, former MLA of the BJP, were also arrested.

Shri Sushil Chandra Verma, Member Of Parliament is reported to have described the present riot in Bhopal as a 'political game'. He criticised the arrest of members of BJP Shri LK Advani, Shri Murali Manohar Joshi and Shri Ashok Singhal. He has appealed to everyone to remain calm and not to leave their residences.

In a statement, Chief Minister Shri Sunder Lal Patwa has appealed to the people to not give credence to rumours and to maintain peace and harmony. He has assured the citizens that the government is taking all necessary steps to ensure their safety and security.

The Chief Secretary Shrimati Nirmala Buch has visited various riot-affected areas and has taken stock of the situation. In Arif Nagar, she has instructed Police to send more security personnels. She has also directed the administration to ensure the security of the citizens and to provide them with all necessary assistance.

Meanwhile, the HRD minister Arjun Singh of Congress (I) has demanded the Governor of Madhya Pradesh Shri Kunwar Mahmood Ali Khan to dissolve the state government, citing its failure to prevent the religious riots. It is said that the Governor is likely to recommend the imposition of President's rule.

In other parts of Madhya Pradesh, curfew has been imposed since yesterday in many areas in Indore, Mhow, Jabalpur, Khandwa, Burhanpur, Ratlam, Jaora, Mominpura, Seoni, Ujjain, Mahidpur, Dewas, Neemuch, Shajapur and Khargone. Prohibitory orders have been imposed in 29 towns of Madhya Pradesh. The situation is said to be largely under control...'

I switched off the transistor. My mind was entangled in a web of divergent narratives surrounding the chaotic events in Bhopal. When I think back on those days, I realise how difficult it is to arrive at a conclusion when such a crisis is unfolding. Amidst the cacophony in society, any official version of events, dictated by the government, clashed fiercely with the impassioned accounts from my staff, what the newspapers said, and the general public's views.

Back then, caught in this whirlwind of perspectives, I couldn't shake the belief that the elusive truth resided in the delicate balance between all these versions, somewhat reminiscent of the adage that in every argument, three facets emerge—your view, my view, and the profound essence of truth. The realisation helped illuminate my path. Anybody who comprehends this intricate interplay can find solace amidst chaos. Just then, Dori Lal entered my room and placed a slip of paper on the table. It said that Uttam Sharma and RK Shinde wanted to meet me. Shinde was the leader of the union that rivals Dada's union, so I was surprised they were visiting together. I asked Dori Lal to send them in after I had finished my call to CGM Gupta and Gokul Singh, to report the events of the previous night.

I called Gupta first. 'Hello, Gupta here,' the deep, husky voice on the other end of the line boomed.

'Good morning, Sir,' I said a little nervous, 'I must report something important.'

'Go ahead,' he replied in his usual commanding voice.

'Last night, there was an attempt of sabotage in the exchange. I thought it was crucial to inform you about it,' I stammered.

'What happened?' he sounded alarmed.

'Sir, it appears that our suspended operator, AW Hassan, who was involved with the saboteurs initially, had a change of heart,' I explained excitedly.

'Interesting,' Gupta replied, sounding intrigued, 'tell me more about it.'

I prepared to reveal the astonishing sequence of events. 'Well, Sir, four individuals planned the sabotage, apparently because their emotions were running high due to the demolition of the Babri Masjid. They managed to infiltrate the exchange by jumping over the fence. AW Hassan was one of them,' I said.

'Go on,' Gupta urged, his voice carrying a mix of anticipation and concern.

'Their intentions were clear; to disrupt our operations and cause chaos. The first blow came when they targeted the transformer fuse, effectively plunging the exchange into darkness,' I said, adding, 'but during this chaos, something remarkable happened. Hassan found himself torn between his initial involvement with the rioters and his loyalty towards our organisation. Seeing the consequences of their hostile actions, realisation dawned upon him.'

'What happened next?'

'Hassan had a change of heart, Sir,' I declared, admiration lacing my words, 'he understood that his actions were not only jeopardising the exchange but also the livelihoods of countless others—including him.'

There was a brief pause as Gupta absorbed the news of Hassan's transformation. 'This is an unexpected event,' he finally remarked.

'Yes, Sir,' I agreed, continuing, 'Hassan's timely realisation showcases his courage and willingness to rectify his mistake. He bravely chose loyalty over misguided emotions, and, in doing so, he prevented further damage to the organisation.'

'It takes courage to admit one's mistake and rectify it. We should commend his change of heart and willingness to protect the organisation,' Gupta said.

'Yes, Sir,' I replied, feeling relieved, 'I believe Hassan's suspension should be reconsidered, as he has demonstrated his commitment to the organisation's well-being.'

'I concur,' Gupta said, 'revoke his suspension and reinstate him immediately. We should acknowledge his loyalty and dedication and arrange a meeting with him to discuss his future prospects.'

'Thank you, Sir,' I responded gratefully, my admiration for Gupta was bolstered.

'Remember,' Gupta added, 'always value employees and nurture their sense of pride in their work. This incident tells us how important the livelihood our organisation provides is to them.'

'Yes, Sir,' I affirmed, feeling a renewed sense of purpose, 'I will ensure Hassan gets the support he needs to thrive in our organisation.'

'Very well,' Gupta concluded, 'and well done.'

'Thank you, Sir,' I said, ending the call.

I had a similar conversation with Gokul Singh, my immediate superior. To my delight, he, too, acknowledged our efforts and agreed to revoke Hassan's suspension. Then he said playfully in Punjabi, '*Ate mainu daso, tusi aj vi exchange de adhina ikale ho. Koi hor adhikari duty wich nahi aaya. Tusi har roz hero ban rahey ho.*' (Are you the only officer on duty at the exchange? No other officer comes these days, so you are becoming a hero every day.)

I burst into laughter, and then said, 'No, Sir. Yesterday, an Assistant Engineer, Nayak, came on duty. And today, Ghosh, Manmohan Singh, and Parvez are on duty. That's why I am relatively free.'

'*Phir tusi aj ghar chaley jao. Yaki tuada man ithe saita hai? Mrs Shrivastava nal koi jhagra toh nahi si?*' he continued to joke. (Then go home today. Or do you like being at office more? Have you fought with Mrs Shrivastava?)

'No, Sir, there's been no argument,' I chuckled. 'I will go home today I will go home,' I said. And he disconnected the call.

Little did I know at that moment how challenging the day was about to become. Uttam and Shinde had been waiting for quite some time. I asked Dori Lal to send them in. As they entered, I gestured towards the sofa and, rising from my chair, stepped forward and extended my hand. We exchanged warm handshakes as a sense of camaraderie pervaded the air. Settling down beside them, I inquired, 'What brings two comrades from opposite poles together?' The term 'comrade' is used affectionately among union associates, fostering a bond of solidarity and shared purpose.

Almost in unison, they burst into giggles. 'Sir, first and foremost, we must credit you for the protection of our exchange not once, but twice,' they said with broad smiles.

Perplexed, I inquired, 'Twice? What do you mean?'

Shinde's eyes lit up as he elaborated, 'Well, first, thanks to your swift actions the saboteurs were foiled. Then, you made timely arrangements for free diesel to keep our backup batteries running before they ran out.'

A collective chuckle filled the room, momentarily lightening the atmosphere. However, Uttam's expression turned serious, and he leaned toward me, speaking in a sombre tone, 'Sir, now I implore you to read the newspaper,' he said.

'Sharma-ji, you know I don't lend much credence to the printed words of today,' I asserted sceptically.

'But Sir,' Shinde interjected, concerned, 'even if merely half of what is printed is true, we must prepare ourselves for the potential repercussions.'

His words made me pause for a moment to contemplate their meaning. 'What has been reported in the newspapers?' I enquired.

Uttam spoke up again, 'One Hindi newspaper has published a piece with the headline '*Kanya Chhatravas Par Dhawa, Maharani Laxmi Bai College Hostel Se Ladkiyan Izzat Bachate Bhaagti Rahin.*' The headline spoke of allegations of an attack on Maharani Laxmi Bai Girls Hostel and the girls escaping to protect their honour.

'And in an English newspaper, it has been reported that women belonging to one community were subjected to rape and the mutilation of their breasts by people from another community in old Bhopal,' Shinde said.

I realised the immense potential for these news articles to incite heated sentiments and provoke a backlash. 'Oh God,' I exclaimed. 'Is this news accurate?'

Uttam then shared an interesting piece of information. He said, 'Chief Secretary Nirmala Buch dismissed these news reports outright during the evening media briefing. She has said that the government has received no information regarding any such incidents.'

'It is because of these very rumours that the police shot our comrade, Aziz Ahmad,' Shinde exclaimed, his words pouring out with unusual urgency.

'No, Shinde,' Uttam interjected, his voice firm yet not unsympathetic. 'I have heard that Aziz was caught up in the frenzy of the moment, and stabbed three Hindus of Sindhi origin. The police showed up and scattered the mob he was a part of, and then caught up with him. I regret his death, but we cannot overlook the cruel end that three people have met at his hands,' he said.

Just then, a coincidence occurred. Dori Lal entered the room to inform me that Aziz's uncle and younger brother were there to see me. The three of us in my office exchanged glances, bewilderment flickering across our faces. *Why were they here? What do they want? Would they pose any threat? Should I invite them in?* Thoughts raced through my mind, swirling in a chaotic whirlwind. Memories of my time with Aziz in Pune resurfaced, then the realisation that he had allegedly killed three people, and the news of his untimely demise at the hands of the police.

Dori Lal awaited my instructions. He asked, 'Sir, what shall I tell them?' Breaking free from my reverie, I responded, '*Unko andar bulao.*'

The pair was ushered into the room then, one slightly older white-haired man, and the other bearing a striking resemblance to Aziz, but younger. They were dressed in white kurta pyjamas, which were stained in some places. They greeted us with polite aadabs. I requested Dori Lal to bring two more chairs for them.

They sat with hands folded close to their chests, eyes fixed on the floor, and shoulders drooping. Deep lines seemed to have been engraved on their foreheads, revealing their fear and nervousness. I instructed Dori Lal to offer them water, and, though he hesitated for a second, he complied.

Emptying the glass of water in one quick gulp, the older man spoke, introducing himself as Jalal, Aziz's uncle and his companion as Jawed, the brother. Then, Jawed made an effort to compose himself, and said, 'Sir, you know that they have shot my elder brother.'

We looked at the two of them with sympathy. It was clear that Jawed had struggled to utter these words. And he went on, 'Sir, his body is in the mortuary of Hamidia Hospital. We want to take his body and perform his burial rites.'

The uncle said, 'They are not allowing us to go there.'

We exchanged glances again, and then Uttam and Shinde looked at me, as if silently asking, *Can you help them?* Indeed, Uttam had been harbouring misgivings about Aziz's actions. But the argument in the corridor with Aziz seemed to have left him nursing a regret. This feeling would fade over time, but perhaps never disappear. After all, Aziz was no longer there to settle scores or hold a debate. That is why Uttam wanted to be conciliatory, despite his doubts about Aziz. Besides, long years of being a union leader had taught him the fine art of striking a balance between conflicting views.

All these thoughts raced through my mind, each carrying its own weight, and I had to wonder if it is morally justifiable to extend assistance to someone accused of a crime. Should I involve myself in a police case? What about the delicate religious sensitivities of this situation? I came to a resolution: no matter the doubts and uncertainties, the fundamental importance was to extend a helping hand to those in need. It was a matter of humanity, transcending religious or legal complexities.

I silently affirmed my decision to Shinde and Uttam to stand by Aziz's family, for it was the right thing to do. Shinde rose from his seat, gently placed his hands on the shoulders of Jalal and Jawed in reassurance and solidarity. Speaking sincerely, he said in Hindi, 'Anupam Sir will help you.'

Jalal and Jawed's eyes were filling up with tears of gratitude. In that moment, a bond formed between everybody in that room, transcending all the barriers of difference, and we were united in our shared commitment to humanity, ready to take the daunting path that lay ahead.

Uttam still harboured a hint of scepticism, so he posed a question, '*Achcha, pehley ye batao, uss din hua kya tha*?' (But first tell us—what happened that day?)

The visitors glanced at each other and began narrating the incident. Jalal explained first, 'Our house is on an upper floor. A procession of Hindus was passing by, raising slogans, celebrating the demolition of the Babri Masjid.'

'Just then, a group of Muslims arrived, and violence erupted; Muslims had started attacking Hindus.' Jawed said, looking at Uttam.

'Aziz said he would go downstairs and try to meditate between those who were squabbling. He did not like that people were fighting,' Jawed said, looking at me.

'We tried to stop him, but he went downstairs before we could change his mind,' Jalal recounted. 'But once he went downstairs, the Muslims there started hurling abuses at him,' he continued, sadly. Jalal said, choking, that they accused him of tarnishing their religion. He recalled how, in the midst of it all, some Hindus attacked Aziz, and he fell to the ground. Then, in the melee, someone handed him a knife, and in the heat of the moment, the tragedy occurred.

'Just then, the police arrived at the scene, and everyone fled, including Aziz, who ran upstairs and closed the door. The police followed him and started banging on the door of the house,' Jalal said.

Once again, the family pleaded with him to not open the door, but Aziz said he would show them his telephone department ID card, which would protect him.

Jawed struggled to find his voice, and when he spoke, his words were filled with anguish, 'As soon as he opened the door, the police shot at him.' He said that the police then threatened all of them. 'Police said that if we engage in violence, we would meet our end just like Aziz had,' he informed us. Then Jawed concluded the sorrowful tale, in which they rushed Aziz to the Hamidia Hospital, but the doctors said he had already died, and sent his body to the mortuary.

Their story left us feeling uncertain about how to respond and whom to hold accountable. It seemed as though the events were somehow predetermined, unfolding in a way beyond anyone's control. It was challenging to place blame solely on Aziz, as he had tried to mediate in a volatile situation. Simultaneously, we found it difficult to accuse the police without acknowledging the complexities they face in maintaining peace. Perhaps it can just be said that the police should focus on imparting training for greater restraint and sensitivity to their officers in such circumstances.

I told Jalal and Jawed to wait outside, in my personal

assistant's room. Uttam and Shinde accompanied them after I had assigned to them the task of meeting employees and ensuring that they know not to get swayed by rumours.

Meanwhile, I tried to contact the superintendent of Hamidia Hospital, but he was making his rounds. He returned my call within an hour. I explained the situation to him and requested the release of our employee Aziz's body for a proper burial by his family. After reviewing the records, the superintendent informed me that since it was a police case and a curfew has been imposed in the whole city, the District Collector's permission would be required.

I dialled the Collector's number, hoping to obtain this clearance, but to my dismay, he was preoccupied in a meeting with the Chief Minister. Valuable time was slipping away. Jalal and Jawed were growing increasingly restless. They returned to my office, their eyes filled with questioning concern. I was transparent with them, explaining the predicament of the clearance required from the Collector. Eager to help, they suggested that I reach out to the Sadbhavna Manch, a Forum for Harmony, and provided me with a number. With a sense of hope, I dialled the number.

After a few ringtones, a familiar voice carrying an air of authority and experience, broke through the static, saying, 'Hello?' I had heard this voice before, but found it difficult to recall exactly where and when.

'Hello, this is Digvijaya Singh,' the voice echoed through the receiver again.

'Oh, Digvijaya Singh, I mean, Sir, is it you, the former minister? This is Anupam Shrivastava, Divisional Engineer, Telephone Department,' I began. My sentiment at the moment was a blend of hope and desperation.

'Yes, Mr Anupam, this is Digvijaya Singh,' he responded. He confirmed on my enquiring that he was a part of the Sadbhavna Manch, dedicated to ensuring peace prevails in the city of Bhopal.

'Sir,' I said, quickly coming to the point. 'I am in difficulty, and earnestly need your assistance,' I said.

After a brief silence, I heard him say, 'Please continue, Mr Anupam.'

I carefully illustrated the need to retrieve the lifeless body of our operator, Aziz Ahmad, from the sombre confines of the Hamidia Hospital mortuary. With heartfelt conviction, I described the profound anguish of his grieving family, their restless anticipation to perform the final rites, and the bureaucratic obstacles that blocked our way. Digvijaya Singh listened, silently but intently. By the time I finished, he seemed to have grasped the gravity of the situation.

'Mr Anupam, I can understand your situation, and I give you my word that I will provide you with the necessary assistance,' he promised, quite authoritatively. He said he would speak to the Chief Minister on my behalf, and ensure that the required official clearance is provided.

A new glimmer of hope rekindled in my heart.

I expressed my gratitude for his willingness to help, genuinely appreciating his assistance in our darkest hour. Of course, at that time, nobody knew that Digvijaya Singh would one day become the Chief Minister of Madhya Pradesh, and that too for two consecutive terms.

'Thank you, Sir,' I said, sounding relieved. 'Your support means the world to us,' I told him.

He responded, 'Rest assured, Patwa-ji would be more than willing to help. In times of crisis, we transcend political boundaries and unite for the greater good. We shall not allow Aziz Ahmad's body to wait in the mortuary, nor allow his grieving family to endure any more hardship,' he said.

We placed our trust in Digvijaya Singh, believing that his influence would expedite the release of Aziz's body. In this interconnected web of empathy and determination, we waited for his promised update. Within fifteen minutes, I received a call from the newly appointed Collector, Pravesh Sharma, who promptly granted permission to retrieve Aziz's body. He also assured that he would personally instruct the Superintendent of Hamidia Hospital to release the body without delay.

However, there was a condition attached to it. In light of the prevailing situation, no procession would be allowed, and only five pall-bearers would be permitted to assemble during the burial. I swiftly conveyed the news to Aziz's uncle and brother, hoping that they would rush to the hospital. However, to my surprise, they remained motionless, their eyes locked upon each other. They explained why the condition set by the Collector posed a significant challenge. Transporting the body to the nearest qabristan (graveyard) near Peer Gate seemed impractical considering the curfew and the volatile situation in Ibrahimpura, which was severely affected by the riots.

After carefully considering the options, I decided to accompany them to the mortuary in my official jeep. We boarded the vehicle almost immediately, with Aziz's uncle taking the seat next to mine and Jawed settled in the back seat. Equipped with a curfew pass, I embarked on this crucial journey. With the least possible delay, we arrived at the hospital, where we made our way to the office of the Superintendent. After a brief exchange, we received the necessary permission letter and proceeded towards the mortuary, our footsteps echoing in the unbearably quiet corridors.

I quickened my pace, surpassing my usual stride, as Jawed and Jalal struggled to keep up, lagging two steps behind me. The weight of this self-imposed responsibility, which urged me to lead them to the mortuary, sat heavily on my shoulders. A part of me yearned to escape and retreat to the solace of my home. It would be dishonest not to admit that, deep inside, I longed to break free from the situation.

The stench of decomposing corpses filled the building we were entering, and I yearned for the comfort of my daily chores, where the emotional crises of others were not my concern. However, the relentless weight of the unprecedented circumstance refused to release its hold. The more I strove to break free, the more entangled I got in its web.

At the entrance to the mortuary, we were received by an attendant, a slightly plump middle-aged man wearing a white topi. He had an almost lifeless presence. But for the smoke emanating from a beedi he puffed, nothing in this room was in motion—stillness was the way of life in a mortuary. The man's eyes, devoid of discernible emotions, mirrored the detachment that comes with years of dwelling among the deceased. It was as if he had become a mere shell, a walking embodiment of life's fragility amidst the realm of the departed.

I placed the permission letter on the iron table and silently urged Jalal to explain our purpose. Clearing his throat, he began speaking in a sombre tone, 'We have come to collect the body of our brother, so that we may lay him to rest with dignity.'

His voice resonated through the solemn mortuary. The attendant, still engrossed in reading the permission letter, asked gruffly, '*Naam*?'

Jalal responded, 'Jalal'.

The attendant's eyes shifted from the permission letter to us, his red eyes devoid of empathy or compassion. His cold voice sliced the thick air. '*Laash ka naam*?' he demanded the name of the body bluntly, with prolonged emphasis on the word laash, dead body.

'Aziz Ahmad,' replied Jalal, sorrowfully.

'*Kaisey mara tha*?' the attendant enquired the cause of death in his detached tone. Jalal's voice quivered as he struggled to find the right words, the weight of the truth evident in his hesitant response.

'He was shot. By the police,' he said, faltering, his voice trailing off towards the end.

The attendant pushed his iron chair back abruptly, making it screech, and pointed towards an open door. 'Go inside, to the left is a pile of those who were shot. Most of them are Muslim. To the right, you'll find a pile of those who were stabbed with knives or daggers. Most of them are Hindu,' he explained in Hindi.

His words echoed my bitter and frightening experiences of the last three days. I had seen a police force overwhelmed by the unexpectedly severe backlash from the Muslim community on December 7 and 8. On December 9, the veritable free-for-all in old Bhopal ended, as the army had been called in. But the pendulum had swung to the other extreme, and members of the Muslim community had been facing brutalities.

Our feet heavy with trepidation, we entered the darkled mortuary. The room had the silence of a grave, broken only by the distant hum of refrigeration units, though it wasn't as cool as one would expect. The scene before us was chilling and heart-wrenching. Rusty broken stretchers were scattered haphazardly, as if their old metallic frames, too, had succumbed under the weight of the tragedy of Bhopal.

Two piles of shroud-less, lifeless bodies lay on a blood-stained floor. The room bore grim witness to the aftermath of violent frenzy. Some bodies had been placed inside the vaults, but their doors were a feeble barrier between the dead and the living world. Others simply lay exposed. More heaps of corpses awaited final disposal, a haunting reminder of the sheer magnitude of the city's losses. Some of the bodies, stacked one upon the other, bore visible signs of a violent end. The room was chillingly still, contrasting with the chaos outside its walls. The pale glow of dim fluorescent lights cast spooky shadows, accentuating its macabre tableau. The pungent odour of antiseptic mingled with that of the decaying dead assaulted our senses. The stench was overpowering, triggering us to involuntarily retch.

We overflowed with the weight of grief and loss within these walls, as if it held the collective anguish of countless departed souls. This haunting experience was a stark testament to the brutality and senselessness of recent events. The faces of the departed, frozen in eternal repose, silently spoke of the tragic consequences of hatred and unrest. Their once-living presence weighed upon us. We had to retrieve Aziz soon, and grant him the dignity and respect he deserved in his final journey.

Silently, I assessed that approximately 150 lifeless bodies lay scattered across the room, mere remnants of the lives they once lived. Just a day or two ago, these were living human beings, and they might have been passionately chanting Allah-hu-Akbar or Har-Har

Mahadev. Some may have brandished knives, fuelled by hatred and violence. But in death, those differences and conflicts seemed irrelevant, and their lifeless forms lay side by side.

Cold reality threatened to overwhelm me, and the urge to flee the place consumed me. Nausea rose within me in waves, but I gathered myself, summoning all the courage I could muster, and turned towards Jalal and Jawed. The challenging task of locating Aziz amidst the sea of the deceased was theirs. They, too, stood frozen, eyes wide with fear, capturing the tumult of emotions within me. The enormity of their task was apparent, yet they had to press on. In that moment, I knew we drew strength from one another, and meant business. We would navigate this maze of the lifeless to fulfil our duty towards our dead family member and colleague.

A sudden cough made us jump. When we turned instinctively towards the source of the noise, our eyes widened in surprise and unease. It was just the mortuary attendant, who stood there, still looking indifferent. In an outstretched arm, he held out a small piece of paper, which we took from him.

It had 'M-0812/195' written on it.

The number's significance eluded us at first. We glanced back at the attendant, mystified, so he enlightened us with an air of detached nonchalance. 'Every dead body has a number tag tied to its right thumb. 'M' marks a Muslim and 'H' marks a Hindu. This is done so that if no one comes to claim a body, the last rites are performed according to the deceased's religious beliefs by the hospital,' the attendant explained the practicality that governed the mortuary's operations. It reduced lives to numbers and alphabets on labels.

If a morgue was bound to be a chilling realisation of the transience of existence, the processes that operated it were a reminder that even in death, one's identity could shrink under death's impersonal bureaucracy. We thanked the attendant, although his attitude had spread a lingering discomfort. We returned to our solemn task, weighed under by the numbers and their implications.

Jawed and Jalal cautiously scanned lifeless bodies and meticulously examined the right thumb of each corpse in search of Aziz. I was too disoriented to participate in the search. Overwhelmed by morbid thoughts, I leaned against a stretcher for support. I dwelled on how each lifeless form laid out before us represented a unique journey, a tapestry of experiences, and a network of connections, now abruptly severed. Jawed and Jalal's occasional hushed whispers punctuated the silence. Finally, their eyes settled upon a tag. Almost simultaneously, they shifted their gaze towards its lifeless face, and a profound grief washed over them.

It was Aziz, his visage now a deep shade of grey, bore witness to the loss of blood he had endured. I helped them to lift the body on one of the stretchers. Jawed began pushing it as we guided it from the sides. Outside, attendees gave us a form to fill out. We penned the necessary details and took possession of

Aziz's body. The attendant looked at us expectantly. I understood this unwritten body language and handed over Rs 20 to him. For the first time, we saw a hint of smile on the corner of his lips.

I realised that my role in the unfolding drama since this afternoon, which I initially thought was limited to a cameo role, was gradually evolving into that of the lead. Increasingly drawn into the tragedy of Aziz's family's loss, I understood that simply delivering his body wasn't the end of my character's trajectory.

As we reached the parked jeep, Jawed and Jalal looked at me with anticipation. By now, we were communicating more through body language than with words. They needed my help in carrying Aziz to his final resting place. I swung open the back door of the jeep, its hinges creaking softly, as if they were grieving, too. I stepped out of the situation for a fleeting second, noting my human tendency to relate the environment with my emotional turmoil.

Jawed and Jalal carefully lifted Aziz's body and placed it on the floor between the seats. His legs were longer than the limited space within, so Jawed tried to bend his knees, but his stiffened limbs offered resistance. A trickle of blood seeped out from a wound stitched on his stomach, and dripped on the floor of the Jeep. Jawed's eyes filled with sorrow and apology met mine. I closed the door slowly, ensuring that it didn't make contact with the legs of the deceased, wanting to avoid further discomfort to his lifeless form.

On Aziz's final journey, Jalal earnestly requested for us to pass through his house. I had to remind him of the Collector's warning and that we must avoid any procession. I had not forgotten the turmoil unfolding in the riot-affected areas. However, Jalal assured me that he would keep it discreet and only bring two more relatives. Reluctantly, I agreed, guided by the principle of unconditional assistance. A thought crossed my mind: in adversity, true compassion knows no boundaries or limitations.

Jalal leading the way, we crossed the Imam Bara Road towards Chowki Imam Bara. Soon, we arrived at a double-storey house. Jalal and Jawed quickly got out of the vehicle and rushed upstairs, leaving me alone with the lifeless body of Aziz. Flashing memories took me back to a few months ago, when we worked together on the directory project in Pune. I remembered the times we would travel to the Sesa Seat office, Aziz in the back seat. Involuntarily, I looked at the rear seat, almost as if I hoped to see Aziz alive. But it was just his lifeless body on the floor, lying wedged between the back door and front seat.

The roads were deserted, only a police van occasionally passing by, patrolling the area. They ignored the vehicle bearing a Government of India sign. If the police were to stop, explaining the dead body might prove challenging. The wait felt excruciatingly long, and minutes seemed to stretch into hours. Finally, they returned with two others, prepared for the burial.

Jawed told me we would need four people to dig the grave. The two relatives opened the front door of the jeep, entered, crossed the front seat and carefully settled in the back seat, making sure not to touch Aziz. Jawed and Jalal squeezed into the front seat. Again, their silent gazes urged me to drive. In a daze, I mechanically started the vehicle and set off towards the burial ground. The collector's words echoed in my mind: *No more than five individuals should be present during the burial.* I mentally counted us, and debated whether Aziz's lifeless body would be considered the sixth person. Before long, we arrived at the graveyard near Peer Gate, bringing our sombre journey to a halt.

Aziz's relatives gently opened the back door of the jeep. They carefully lifted his lifeless body, legs folded, and laid him on a stone platform. The others began digging his grave, while Jalal and Jawed attended to the body. Jalal had brought a fresh white garment to dress him in. They carefully washed him, and I couldn't help but wonder whether the water was warm or cold, and whether Aziz could feel the chill of that winter evening. I joined them in dressing Aziz in his final attire. Then, they covered him with a white sheet and tied it securely on the corners. Meanwhile, the grave facing in the direction of holy Mecca was ready for him.

All five of us carefully lifted Aziz's body and slowly lowered it into the grave. Tears streamed down Jalal's face. He said that I should place the first handful of soil into the grave. I gathered my strength and placed the soil gently on his body. The other relatives followed suit, slowly filling up the grave with their hands, eventually completing the process with a hoe.

In the end, I looked up at the sky and saw a full moon ascend the horizon, casting an orange glow. It felt as if the moon had carried the essence of Aziz's departed soul, merging him with the ethereal light illuminating this night. One by one, the relatives approached me and hugged me to express their heartfelt gratitude.

After dropping the relatives off along the way, I started to drive back to the office, now my temporary home, satisfied that despite the restrictive curfew and the violence in the city, we had buried Aziz respectfully. It had been an emotionally demanding endeavour, but one that had to be done.

That night, back on the sofa in my office, sleep eluded me. The weight of the day's events and the relentless surges of stress had left me in a state of perpetual restlessness. The haunting mortuary with its cold, sterile walls and lifeless bodies danced before my eyes in frames. I reached for the transistor-clock. It said 11 p.m. and I turned it on, unleashing a symphony of static to fill the room. White noise enveloped me like a gentle embrace from an old friend. It was my feeble attempt to drown out the cacophony of thoughts and anxieties that plagued my every waking moment.

I closed my heavy eyelids, surrendering to the abyss of sleep. There was no solace in my restless slumber, yet, time slowly lost its grip on me, and reality melted away, leaving me alone in the intangible kingdom of the subconscious. It felt as though I was awake, but trapped inside a vivid dream. The day's events unfolded in my subconscious like scenes from a movie. Suddenly, in this dream stage of sleep, my heartrate climbed, and respiration heightened, evoking fear, anxiety, and sadness. I was back in the mortuary, staring at lifeless bodies. In an instant, only four of the corpses remained, those of Aziz and the three people he had killed. All four opened their eyes, making a reflexive shiver to course through me in my wakeful sleep.

The three people Aziz had allegedly killed moved closer to him, and I wondered what their intentions were. Would they seek revenge, even after death? I instinctively tried to intervene to protect him. But then, Aziz greeted all three with a smile, and, to my surprise, the four figures embraced. Their bodies seemed to merge into a radiant white glow of light for a fleeting moment, before separating again. Aziz spoke first, his eyes filled with remorse.

'I didn't even know all of you,' he said in a sorrow-laden voice. 'Then how could some people incite me with their slogans?' he went on.

'We are Rajesh, Dheeraj, and Aman Lal,' Rajesh said with a smile. 'We were orphans who came to Bhopal from our villages in search of livelihoods. We used to work at the Union Carbide factory before the gas tragedy. Afterwards, we became waiters at Naseem Hotel.'

His voice carried a forgiving tone, already accepting the past. Dheeraj, his eyes filled with embarrassment, spoke next. 'We were fervently shouting slogans, fearing that the chants of Har-Har Mahadev would be drowned out by Allah-hu-Akbar,' he said.

Aziz, extending his hands towards them, said, 'I am to blame for your suffering. I don't know what came over me. I was an educated person.'

Then Aman Lal, the third victim, held Aziz's extended hand and reassured him, 'Don't blame yourself. Even after you badly wounded us, we could have survived if someone had taken us to the hospital immediately. But due to the curfew, no ambulance was available, and the hospitals had few doctors. You, too, would have lived if someone had taken you to a hospital after you were shot by the police.'

Aziz sounded astonished as he asked, 'Do you know how I was killed?' In an instant, he realised the futility of asking, for in the world of souls, there is knowledge of the present, past, and future in a unified consciousness, beyond human existence. All four smiled in understanding, their bodies merging into a radiant white glow, then separating again.

Dheeraj whispered regretfully, 'There is a lingering remorse in me, and it is over something nobody understands. The people who brought us to the mortuary were discussing plans to further instigate fear in areas where the Muslims and other communities live. They spoke of wanting to use tape recorders and loudspeakers to spread terror, hoping to provoke more agitation and prolong the riots.'

'*Arey bhai,*' Aman Lal spoke with a mix of frustration, scepticism, and, perhaps, resignation, 'sure, build a temple, but will it mean Ram Rajya in the country?'

'And our *roti, kapda aur makaan* cannot wait indefinitely either…' Rajesh lamented.

Aziz replied with mixed emotions, 'I, too, regret the poverty and backwardness among my community members. If only someone could take up the cause to emancipate and improve their lot, especially the women. *Kya koi aisa raja ayega jo gurbat say hamey uthayega*?' he said. (Will a king ever come who frees us from poverty?) His eyes flashed with longing for such a ruler.

But not for long did they look morose. Their smiles returned soon, and Rajesh held Aziz and Dheeraj then turned to Aman Lal, who asked, 'So, what do we say now? Har-Har Mahadev? Allah-hu-Akbar? Or *Hindu-Muslim-Sikh-Issai, aapas me sab bhai-bhai*?'

His plea for unity and harmony among faiths had barely escaped his lips when they suddenly became aware of my presence and turned towards me. They look serene and wise. I felt new energy coursing from their collective consciousness, enveloping me and merging with my being. I was experiencing a profound connection with something much bigger than myself. Then the piercing screams of a mob and distant gunfire abruptly pulled me out of my dream, smashing the tranquillity I had been feeling.

Momentarily disoriented, I lost all sense of my surroundings. Gradually, the white noise emanating from the transistor, which had lulled me into a deep, deep slumber, brought me back to the present, grounding me back in reality.

ज़िन्दगी हँसने गाने के लिए है पल दो पल
ज़िन्दगी हँसने गाने के लिए है पल दो पल
इसे खोना नहीं खो के रोना नहीं
इसे खोना नहीं खो के रोना नहीं

Life is to laugh and sing
For a moment or two
To laugh and sing
For a moment or two
Don't lose it, and don't cry if it is lost
Don't lose it, and don't cry if it is lost.

CHAPTER SEVEN

Rocks and Bottles

December 10

Emerging from the City Exchange building and turning left onto the main road, I drove the jeep through the quiet streets of Bhopal. The peppy melody of a cheerful Hindi song from the Sony cassette player in my jeep helped in keeping the mood light. The poignant lyrics aptly represented the essence of life's ups and downs. I was driving my trusty blue Mahindra jeep, surrounded by the desolate emptiness of the evening on December 10, 1992.

After four long days, I was finally headed back to my humble abode in the Arera Colony, having spent countless hours in the City Exchange building. Throughout these exhausting days, I had managed to catch only a few hours of sleep each night, on the makeshift office sofa. Emptiness and unease drowned out my relief, as my sights fell upon the majestic Taj-ul-Masjid, which stood proudly to my left. The grand structure, known for its serene presence in the city, conveyed an uncertain future.

Rumours whispered over those four days had made the tranquillity of the mosque doubtful. They claimed that Pakistani citizens had sought refuge within its sacred walls, and that a stockpile of arms lay hidden within its premises—an alleged 'tanker-load of gunpowder'. These unsettling rumours made the respected sanctuary a suspected site, leaving people to grapple with the concern and disbelief it now evoked. The Taj-ul-Masjid, which typically bustled with devoted worshippers and international visitors, especially during the annual Islamic ijtema, was eerily quiet. As if holding its breath, it waited for the violence to subside. I heard slogans and gun-shots in the distance, but within the mosque, the soft shuffling of footsteps, the gentle unfurling of prayer rugs, and the hushed murmurs of prayer filled the air. The mosque seemed to absorb the chaotic sounds of the world it stood in, standing as a beacon of oceanic repose amidst stormy waves. As one of the largest and a renowned mosque, it had always earned the admiration of visitors to Bhopal. Its construction began in the late 19th century under the rule of Sultan Shah Jahan Begum, but was halted for almost 20 years, until it resumed under the rule of her daughter, Sultan Kaikhusrau Jahan Begum and later builders, and was finally completed in 1958.

Its three huge domes and two towering minarets

that are 206 feet high were constructed in the Indo-Islamic architectural style with a vast courtyard and a spacious prayer hall that can accommodate thousands of worshippers. Its marvellous Quranic calligraphy and intricate patterns on walls, pillars, and ceilings, impressed every visitor. The main entrance was adorned with two grand arches with beautiful carvings. As I drove past it, my gaze involuntarily turned towards it, searching for the tanker filled with explosives or armed foreign mercenaries! Stories circulated in newspapers had affected a part of me, creating a lingering doubt. But as I watched, the mosque seemed to understand my apprehensions and, in response, its loudspeaker released the maghrib prayer call, which echoed in the barren street.

The mellow prayer-call unexpectedly filtered into the jeep despite the loud music I was playing. Was it my imagination? But I focused my attention, and realised that the prayer call's melody was real and tangible inside the jeep. A harmonious fusion of the music and prayer formed a unique and captivating symphony. The lyrics of the song that had held special significance for me just moments ago was eclipsed by the profound power and magnificence of the muezzin's call. It was just a fleeting moment or two, but it quelled the restlessness within me, and I felt serene and composed. A calmness took over my mind for now, and the cassette player reminded me of the importance of laughter and music.

The last stanza of the song that I had played on the cassette player now chimed in:

प्यारे तू ग़म न कर
ज़िन्दगी हॅसने-गाने के लिए है
पल दो पल
ज़िन्दगी हॅसने-गाने के लिए है
पल दो पल...

(Worry not, dear
For life is to laugh and sing
For a moment or two
Life is to laugh and sing
For a moment or two.)

My hands gripped the steering wheel tight on the eerily empty streets, and ejected the cassette, preferring silence for the curfewed day. Inevitably, the silence created space in my mind to recollect the scene in the morgue, of lifeless bodies piled like furniture. The morgue was too vivid, raw, and painful an experience to brush off easily. That room personified the anger, the hatred, and the violence that can make humans savage. What if those scenes, smells and sounds never escaped my psyche, I wondered. The long-term adverse effects of having lived through traumatic events was notoriously hard for individuals to fathom.

The road ahead was bumpy and uneven, just like my thoughts and emotions, which swayed and jumped on every pothole and crack in the experiences of the last few days. But the suspension of the jeep I drove was in no way comparable to the plush drive quality of today's cars. It was a roller coaster ride in every way, but my feelings were worse off than the vehicle. I felt like I was in a storm at sea, high with adrenaline one moment, then crashing down a tidal surge, fearful and uncertain. As I steered a corner, driving around the main gate of Gandhi Medical College, I saw a group of police officers standing by the roadside, their guns drawn and ready. My heart rate quickened as I approached them, but they waved me through without a second glance. I felt grateful again for the 'Government of India' sign on my vehicle. I honked to reciprocate their free pass and even slowed a bit, out of empathy for their selfless service in the midst of the chaos and violence.

The police symbolise hope and order, and protection of the innocent and of peace in the city. Amidst destruction and fear, their presence is a beacon of light, a reminder that even in dark times, some will stand up for what is right. The initial two days of the rioting had been chaotic, and the police force was greatly outnumbered by the relentless onslaught of miscreants. They even had to endure beatings, and an escalating crisis of violence, which meant they had to respond with force, including firearms. One could even say that tit for tat is their only mantra. But once miliary reinforcements arrived, the balance of power shifted, and order was restored to a very large extent, at least in old Bhopal.

I swept my eyes across both sides of the road,

revealing closed doors that once bustled with market activities. It was still a ghost town. Bhopal, my hometown, which I held dear, had transformed into a conflict zone, bringing immense suffering to its people. I wanted desperately to take action, contribute towards restoring justice and peace. I yearned to make a difference, offer my assistance in any way possible. Yet, my role was confined to that of mere observer, driving slowly to my cherished home. I held onto the flickering hope that this ride would end my worries, too.

But the unfolding drama would soon extend its arms into the confines of my family sanctuary. I noticed the Imambara Road, which led to Chowki Imam Bara, inhabited predominantly by Muslims and severely impacted by the riots. Here, too, the scene was of silence and desolation. The abandoned street was blanketed by the heavy weight of a curfew. Somewhere here, Aziz had once lived, his life cut short. All at once, the chilly air penetrated my bones, making me break into a cold sweat. The sensation was all too familiar after the events of yesterday. Anxiety had embraced me tight, and formed a knot around my chest that refused to loosen.

Each passing moment was filled with the rattles and bumps of dodging the potholes and debris strewn on the roads. Abruptly, I slammed on the brakes as my mind was gripped by an inexplicable impulse.

Melancholy began to dissipate again, as hope

flickered, even feelings of peace and being close to divinity. An ethereal force now seemed to guide me, and I believed it was towards a place of serenity. It began as a mere whisper in the recesses of my mind, with a gentle reassurance that everything would be alright. I took deep breaths, renewing the calmness I felt. I could taste equanimity in the very air I inhaled.

And there it was, my destination, the captivatingly named Curfew Wali Mata temple, a majestic embodiment of motherly love and protection. In the stillness, the temple radiated more than its time-honoured grandeur. The intricate carvings embellishing its walls, and the illuminated statue of Mata Rani I had seen many times, captivated my mind's eye. The sun had begun its descent, casting golden and crimson hues upon the sky, an exquisite tapestry stretching into eternity. Against this breathtaking panorama, I saw the divine mother stand tall, her statue embraced by the radiant glow of the setting sun. She looked awakened, suffused with the divine essence that set her apart from this world. In her presence, I felt awestruck and my heart filled with reverence. It was a moment to recognise the divinity that innately resides in all of us.

Stepping out of the jeep, I stood before the temple, and nobody was in sight. Seeking solace, I entered, silently closing my eyes. Perhaps it was exhaustion or maybe, I just needed to sleep, but I settled down against one of the temple's pillars. I rested my head and back against its cool stone. The only sound I could hear was my breathing and the gentle breeze that caressed my face like a loved one's whispers. Suddenly, I felt a presence around me. I opened my eyes and saw Devi Mata standing there, right in front of me, her divine, serene face looking at me kindly.

'Who are you?' I asked, bewildered. I looked around, not from fear, but to quickly take in the ambience. I noticed that everything around me had changed. My jeep had disappeared, and even the dark, silent buildings around the temple had vanished. A soothing white light sheathed me then, seemingly protecting me from everything chaotic and noisy that was happening in the world. I was in a trance-like state.

'I am your Divine Mother,' she replied.

Taken aback, I could only say, 'Devi Mata, what brings you here?'

'Your confusion has summoned me,' she said, gentle and soothing, adding, 'You seek some answers.'

I quivered, amazed that a divine being had understood my quest.

'What troubles you?' Devi Mata asked.

'Why do people harbour hatred for one another?' I asked her with sadness, 'what is the purpose of religion if it fails to unite people?'

Devi Mata regarded me benevolently, and then said, 'Religion is not the reason for divisions, child. Its purpose is to unite us in shared humanity, and guide us to find the meaning and purpose of life.'

'If so, why do people fight in the name of religion?'

I asked, even more perplexed.

'People fight because they are driven by fear,' Devi Mata said. 'They fear change and the unknown. It gets worse when those who seek power and control wield religion as their tool. However, people can rise above their differences and transcend their ego, and we can create a harmonious and peaceful world,' she said.

'But, Devi Mata,' I said, 'why is there so much violence when people get religiously provoked?'

'Conflicts and bloodshed are sparked by the desire for control, but religion promotes love, compassion, and peace. It is a path to connect with the divine and discover our true nature,' Devi Mata replied.

'So, why do we have different beliefs and practices?' I inquired.

'The diversity of religion is just a reflection of diverse cultures, histories and circumstances. They are just different paths to connect with the divine,' she said.

'Can't we achieve this without religion?' I asked.

'Of course,' said the goddess. 'Religion is not the only way, 'but it is a valid approach for many. The other ways can be communion with nature, or through art, love, and service. Religion offers a framework, a structure, a community, and practices that can help us get there,' she said.

I wanted to understand my role in this world, so I gathered courage and asked, 'Devi Mata, what is my purpose for existing?'

She said, 'Your purpose is unique to you. Each soul

has its own path and contribution to offer. Your role in this world is to discover your true self, to cultivate love, compassion, and kindness, and to share your gifts and talents for humanity. A divine spark lives within you, and your life's journey is about discovering it and letting it shine brightly.'

I blinked, trying to comprehend the profound meaning of these words. Sensing my confusion, she continued, 'But while you have the right to fulfil your duties, you are not entitled to the outcomes. So, do not become attached to inaction or lethargy.'

She pointed her divine finger at me. 'Right now, your duty is to ensure the telephone facilities work, unaffected by circumstances, and to not get consumed by circumstances, or the notions of whether you will get success, reward, or recognition.'

'Remember,' she said, touching my forehead, 'the journey towards enlightenment is long and winding, but I will guide your way.'

I thanked Devi Mata profusely, and she slowly faded away, followed by the gentle white light leaving, but my trance-like state did not lift for some time. I wanted to never leave that state of tranquillity. Then, like a bolt from the blue, the wail of a police siren broke my reverie.

Disoriented, I looked around again, and saw a police vehicle, its lights flashing. Its siren rang in my ears again, like a splash of cold water. The soothing light had receded, and I was back in the familiar world.

The vanished buildings and my jeep also materialised before my eyes. The police car was just speeding past, and its siren faded away into the distance. I realised that I was sitting inside a temple in the midst of a curfew all over the city.

Much later, I learnt why the Mata Rani temple had such an unusual name, Curfew Wali Mata temple. It is an enthralling tale linked with the temple's existence. This temple emerged during a period of heightened unrest and curfews in the city in the year 1981. Even before its construction began, a sacred statue of Mata Rani was installed during the auspicious festival of Navratri. However, as the situation escalated, the government issued an order to halt all construction. The dispute between the people and the authorities reached such a fervent crescendo that a curfew was imposed upon the city for fourteen arduous days.

Undeterred by the obstacles before them, the devoted populace persevered with determination, and eventually, their efforts bore fruit. The temple stood tall, a testament to their unwavering faith and indomitable spirit. It came to be known as the Curfew Wali Mata Temple, becoming the epicentre of devotion for countless worshippers. The devotees firmly believed that with a coconut, carefully wrapped and offered to Mata Rani, their deepest desires and aspirations would be granted. In times of strife, particularly during curfews and other adversities, the temple transformed into a sanctuary of solace and hope for the people of Bhopal. It became a symbol of their faith, determination, and unyielding perseverance.

But that day, with the image of Devi Mata fresh in my mind, I turned away from the temple and trudged back to my jeep. Every step felt like it was taken in a dream, and I wished that I could stay where I was for some more time in an absolute state of peace and divinity. As I reached the jeep, I weighed my options for a moment. Then I climbed into the driver's seat. The world seemed distant and unreal, as if I were watching it through a veil. But I knew that I had to keep going and do my duty.

With a deep breath, I turned the key in the ignition, the engine roared to life. The familiar sound of the Jeep's powerful rumble provided a comforting diversion from my thoughts. With renewed vigour, I engaged the gear and swiftly manoeuvred around the corner, leaving behind the vicinity of Bada Talab at Ret Ghat Chauraha and the MPEB station, which I had visited only two days prior in the dead of the night.

A short distance ahead, my attention was captivated by a vibrant green structure standing prominently in the middle of the road. It was the Chameli Wale Baba ki Dargah, a revered place of worship for Muslims and people of other faiths. I had been told tales of Hindus and Christians alike, who sought solace and offered prayers at this serene sanctuary during times of hardship. Legends surrounding the dargah even spoke of it being the final resting place of the cherished mare of Chameli Wale Baba. As part of my daily commute, I would nod in respect each time I passed by, acknowledging its significance.

On busy days, the flow of traffic was redirected to accommodate the presence of the dargah, allowing it to stand as a symbol of hope and unity amidst the bustling chaos. Vehicles manoeuvred around the sacred site, acknowledging its sanctity and embracing the spirit of coexistence. As I drove past the majestic dargah, an overwhelming urge compelled me to find a place to pause and contemplate my extraordinary encounter with Devi Mata. Did it truly happen? Did I really witness the divine presence of Devi Mata? Lost in deep thought, I unconsciously steered the wheel to the right, leading me towards the enchanting Bada Talab, a renowned lake that has always been a source of pride for the residents of the city of Bhopal. Its beauty and significance are ingrained in the hearts of its inhabitants, and there is a famous saying associated with its splendour: Talon mein tal Bhopal tal, baqi sab tallaiya. It means that Bada Talab is the only lake worth the name; all others are mere ponds in comparison.

Bada Talab, also known as the Upper Lake, the large artificial lake in the heart of Bhopal, symbolised the diversity of Bhopal and always inspired its people. Surrounded as it is by numerous temples, mosques, and other religious sites, and visited by people belonging to all faiths, it became a symbol of unity and religious harmony. Its history goes back to the 11th century, when the Parmara king Bhoj constructed a dam on the Kolans River, creating the lake. Originally, it was a source of water for the city of Bhojpal, which was later renamed Bhopal. During the reign of the Mughal emperor Aurangzeb, Bhopal was granted to the Nawab of Bhopal. In the 18th century, a new dam was constructed to increase its capacity. In the early 20th century, the British made several improvements to it, including a new water treatment plant and a modern water supply system.

I interrupted my journey towards my home and pulled over on the side of Bada Talab. I surveyed the vast expanse of water, and a profound sense of calm washed over me as I took in the stillness of the water and the serene landscape. On the drive from Bhopal city towards Van Vihar, a popular national park, I had often passed by this water body. Driving along its edges, I had enjoyed the panoramic views of its waters and the hills flanking it to the west. The highway along it created a scenic route, a serene driving experience away from the hustle and bustle of the city, especially during the sunset and twilight.

The beauty of the lake overwhelmed me that evening, momentarily rendering me speechless. The sun was setting over the lake, casting a breathtaking array of colours across the water. The shades of orange, crimson, and pink blended with hints of red and purple, painted a mesmerising backdrop. The shimmering waters mirrored these hues, creating a visual spectacle. The peacefulness was enhanced by a gentle breeze that caressed the surface of the lake, making ripples form. The peaceful natural ambience accompanied by the melodic chirping of birds created a soothing and calming atmosphere, unaffected by the city's rush of activity. It was a respite from the world. Lost in thoughts, I pondered the profound words of Devi Mata, assuring me of her eternal presence as my guardian angel. Suddenly, a gentle breeze brushed my hair, carrying with it a touch of coolness. A deep sense of connection enveloped me, and I felt Her divine presence comforting and guiding me.

On the rest of the drive home, a feeling of contentment enveloped me, and a joyful tune escaped my lips in a whistle. The familiar streets guided me effortlessly, and, before I knew it, I had arrived at the entrance gate of my house. The sun had already set and the day had begun its descent into twilight. Traces of daylight clung to the edges of the sky, gradually giving way to the encroaching darkness.

To my astonishment, I spotted my father anxiously securing the premises of our house, clutching the 12-bore rifle tight. His actions conveyed an urgency and concern, which immediately caught my attention. As I approached the gate, he swiftly swung it open, gesturing for me to enter swiftly. I stepped out of the jeep, and my father hurriedly locked the gate, never loosening his firm grip on his rifle. His expression revealed a mixture of worry and determination, leaving me eager to understand the reason behind his evidently distressed demeanour.

'Come inside the house, son, quickly,' he urged, guiding me towards the entrance.

'What's going on, Papa?' I inquired.

'Our colony is under attack by armed men from the Muslim community,' he revealed, his voice quivering with apprehension.

'From where? How do you know? Who told you?' I bombarded him with questions, desperately trying to make sense of the situation.

As I stepped over the threshold, my father swiftly secured the door behind us, sealing us off from the world. The air was filled with anticipation as my sons darted towards me, their voices echoing off the walls, 'Papa is home, Papa is home,' their tiny hands clinging to my legs with unbridled excitement.

My heart overflowing with love, I scooped them up in my arms, and their giggles filled the room. My wife stood nearby, wearing a shy smile, joy gleaming in her eyes. Mindful of my father's presence, I embraced her in a tender side hug, cherishing the warmth between us. Just then, my mother emerged from her room, staring intently at me. A fleeting expression of concern crossed her features as she noticed my stubble, evidence of the days that had passed. Her voice trembled with worry as she voiced her apprehension over my apparent loss of weight.

Gently placing the children back on their feet, I bowed respectfully and touched my mother's feet, a gesture of reverence ingrained in tradition. In that moment, all other thoughts vanished, and I was consumed by the soothing embrace of my home, cocooned in its familiar warmth and the love that resided within its walls.

I turned towards my father, his eyes glued on the road as he took a chair in the drawing room, the rifle still in his hands. My sons clambered onto my lap as I took the chair beside him, one sitting on each leg. With innocent curiosity, they reached out to touch my four-day-old beard, their eyes filled with wonder. My wife and mother had retreated into the kitchen, preparing a much-needed repast of tea and snacks.

I inquired again, 'Papa, why are you holding the rifle? What is happening?'

My father's eyes briefly shifted from the window to meet mine and he said, 'Our colony is under attack.'

'An attack? Who could be responsible for this?' I questioned, my mind racing to comprehend the situation.

His eyes scanned the darkness outside, as he recounted the events, 'There was a loud commotion coming from the direction you drove your jeep. I could hear hundreds of people shouting Allah-hu-Akbar, accompanied by the desperate screams of others.'

As he spoke, I glanced outside the window, but the dimly-lit road struggled to cast light on the scene my father had described. A foreboding hung in the air.

I chuckled softly then, the amusement in my voice evident. 'It seems you may have jumped to conclusions, Papa,' I remarked.

'The road I drove on was utterly empty, devoid of any sign of activity or people. There was no immediate threat or disturbance in that direction.' Glancing outside again, I reaffirmed the emptiness of the streets. My sons, their eyes filled with concern, observed our conversation intently.

Suddenly, my wife and mother's voices resonated from the kitchen, in tones filled with alarm. 'We heard the commotion and the frightening shouts, too!' they exclaimed in unison.

I turned towards my father, who, with a hint of sarcasm, said, 'See? And you don't believe me. We've been hearing these slogans and terrifying noises every night. But how would you know? You haven't been home for four days.'

I couldn't help but suppress a full-blown laugh. 'I understand, Papa,' I said, trying to compose myself. Then I explained: 'There is a group of troublemakers in the city. They drive around in a Maruti Van equipped with loudspeakers and tape recorders. At every corner they across, they stop the vehicle for a few seconds and play these cassettes at full volume, creating panic among people.'

My father's stern expression deepened as he responded with disbelief and concern, 'I find it hard to believe that it's as simple as that. These voices, to me, sound like an approaching mob, ready to attack.'

'They are instigators, deliberately stoking strife between people,' I interjected, unable to conceal my frustration. 'Their interests lie in perpetuating division among communities. They deliberately target Hindu neighbourhoods, blaring these cassettes with Allah-hu-Akbar chants through their loudspeakers, creating the illusion of a Muslim mob rampaging nearby. And then they visit Muslim localities, playing cassettes with chants of Har-Har Mahadev, as if Hindus are about to pounce on Muslims and attack them.'

My mother and wife, with concerned expressions, joined the conversation, placing cups of tea and my favourite snack, poha, on the table in front of me. 'It's absolutely deplorable that such individuals exist, sowing discord for their sinister agendas,' my wife said, her voice trembling with emotion.

Then, my younger son babbled in babytalk: 'Papa, *yeh Allah-hu-Akbar aur Har-Har Mahadev kya hotey hain?*'

My elder son, displaying the wisdom of his five years, quickly responded on my behalf, 'Don't you know even this much? It means that Hindus, Muslims, Sikhs and Christians are brothers and sisters.'

Everyone shared a heartfelt laugh at the children's pure understanding of unity and love. The pressure in the room dissipated and my father set aside his rifle, looking relieved. Yet, my mind couldn't help but drift back to the vivid dream I had had recently, where a similar message of unity was delivered from the ethereal realms. I longed for my children to retain their innocence always, to remain shielded from the harsh realities that permeate the adult world, rife with violence and senseless acts.

A worry gripped me, as I realised that Bobby was nowhere to be seen. Concerned, I turned to my father and urgently inquired, 'Papa, where is Bobby?'

My parents exchanged a brief glance filled with hesitation and apprehension. It was my mother who spoke up, her voice sounding anxious, 'He is upstairs on the terrace, keeping a watchful eye over the house.'

'Watchful eyes? Against what?' I asked.

'Yes, for the past few nights, he has taken it upon himself to guard the terrace under the recess of the water tank,' my father explained, his tone failing to conceal his admiration. 'He does it as a precautionary measure if there is any attack from the people of other faiths,' he added.

I found it difficult to comprehend the need for such vigilance, especially considering where we lived, one of the safest neighbourhoods in Bhopal. But explaining this to my family proved challenging. I decided to address the matter later. After a refreshing hot shower and shave, I made my way to the dining table for our first family meal in four days. Bobby was already at the table, engrossed in his contemplations, eating mechanically. As he noticed me, he stood up and gave me a brief hug before returning to his meal. Within minutes, he swiftly pushed back his chair and excused himself. I called out to him: 'Bobby, come here. I'd like to discuss what's been happening lately,' attempting to strike up a conversation.

'Bhai Sahab, you won't understand, since you're hardly ever at home, always occupied with your office work,' he retorted, annoyed. 'Our colony is under attack, and there's a looming threat of rioters vandalising our homes,' he added, his tone brimming with frustration.

'I was doing my duty, Bobby. I was present in the worst riot-affected areas. Many lives were lost due to stabbings and in police firing,' I tried to express my perspective.

'Yes, that's the difference, Bhai Sahab. Hindus are slaughtered while Muslims die in police firing,' my brother replied, his agitation palpable. 'We Hindus are defenceless without the protection of the police. That's why we have made the decision to rise and protect ourselves,' he added, pride resonating in his voice.

'We?' I echoed, surprise evident in my voice. 'Who are "we"?' Have you formed a local militia or something, hmm?' I enquired, trying to make sense of his statement.

'Not a local militia, Bhai Sahab, but we are a group of individuals who remain vigilant and protect our houses from our rooftops,' he explained. 'Finish your dinner and come to the terrace, and I'll show you,' he added, anticipation in his voice.

I quickly finished dinner and ascended the two flights of stairs outside our house and emerged on the rooftop. Bobby, still in his early twenties, had surrounded himself with a collection of stones and soda bottles, all concealed beneath the recess of the water tank. A small mattress, a thick duvet, a pocket transistor, and a container of water were also placed nearby. He stood there proudly, ready to explain his strategy.

'This is our defence, Bhai Sahab,' he proclaimed with conviction. 'If the rioters come, I will throw stones and soda bottles at them, making them run away in fear.'

I stood, unsure how to react. I appreciated his concern for the safety of our home and family, but I couldn't help but feel uneasy about this seemingly immature and unnecessary arrangement. I knew, first and foremost, that there was no threat to us. And, even if there was, confronting a violent situation like this would require more than throwing stones and soda bottles.

'Bobby,' I began, cautiously, 'I understand your intentions, but when a real adversity of this kind comes, it requires a different kind of preparedness and resilience to face it. Moreover, I have information that there is no immediate threat in New Bhopal,' I said, trying to convince him.

He was silent for a moment, his gaze distant as he attempted to process and—I could see—dismiss my words. Suddenly, he sprang to his feet, a burst of energy propelling him forward, and he released a resounding cry, 'Jagtey raho.' (Be vigilant.) His cry reverberated through the chilly winter night, reaching the ears of others in nearly thirty houses, who responded in unison, 'Jagtey raho'.

I realised that his determination to protect our community was unwavering. I reflected on the situation and felt a pang of sadness. It seemed that, despite our efforts, the divisions within society had become deeply entrenched. The success of interested groups in polarising communities for political gain had created an atmosphere of mistrust and suspicion. It was disheartening to see how fake news and the deliberate dissemination of inflammatory messages through loudspeakers had gained more credibility than attempts at reconciliation. In the bewildering realm of riots in Bhopal, a concerning trend prevailed where fake news appeared real, while real news grew feeble-voiced.

I looked up at the night sky. The first waning moon had begun its ascent on the eastern horizon, casting a soft, ethereal glow upon the world. In that moment, a glimmer of hope flickered within me. I yearned for a future where the voices of understanding, compassion, and harmony would drown out the divisive cacophony of the loudspeakers. A future where people possessed the discernment to differentiate between real news and false news.

With slow, weary steps, I descended the staircase.

The exhaustion of the past four days weighed heavily on my shoulders. Upon reaching my bedroom, I found my wife and our two sons eagerly waiting for me. As I settled into bed, my boys nestled on either side, their faces filled with anticipation. They insisted on hearing their favourite bedtime story, the same one that I had told them countless times. I began narrating the tale of Chho She, Ba She and Ba Ba She, but before I could complete the first sentence, fatigue overcame me, and I drifted into peaceful slumber. In what felt like a mere instant, I was shaken awake by my wife. The persistent ringing of the telephone in my dream now transformed into the incessant chiming of the doorbell.

Still startled, but I hastily made my way towards the main door, emerging from their bedroom, my father and mother close behind. On the other side, my brother's voice was filled with urgency and desperation, pleading for us to open the door without delay. With a mix of confusion and concern, I swiftly unlatched the door, allowing my brother to rush inside. He slammed the door shut behind himself, seeking refuge inside the home. Without uttering a word, he hurriedly went to his room, and cocooned himself within the warmth of a duvet. Tremors wracked his body as we anxiously bombarded him with questions, eager to understand the events that unfolded on the terrace.

Collecting himself, he began to explain what had transpired. 'It was almost midnight, and I was lying on the terrace, listening to music on the transistor with the volume turned down low. I was mentally prepared to react quickly if I heard voices below, which would mean that the rioters had arrived,' he whispered.

We had all turned our attention towards him, my mother was seated beside him, her hand gently placed on his head, and my father sat across her, holding his hand to provide comfort. 'All of a sudden, I heard some unsettling conversation from our neighbour's rooftop,' he continued.

'Cautiously, I approached the edge of our rooftop, where a parapet wall separates us from our neighbours, and I saw a few people searching for something,' he recounted. 'I thought they were rioters and that our neighbourhood was under attack,' he mumbled. 'But, to my surprise, they were armed policemen, and they saw me,' he revealed.

As he continued his account, we were all captivated, hanging onto his every word. 'The policemen turned towards me with expressions of surprise. In that tense moment, they raised their guns and shouted at the top of their lungs, demanding to know who was there,' he recalled. 'Fear gripped me, for I felt sure that they were about to shoot at me, so I sprinted down the stairs, taking two or three steps at a time,' he said, the memory of that terrifying moment still fresh in his mind. He pleaded in a voice filled with worry, 'Bhai Sahab, what if the policemen come to our house looking for me? Please assure them that I was on the terrace out of curiosity. They must not see the stones and soda water bottles collected there.'

'Don't worry, Bobby. Nothing will happen, and I will handle the situation if policemen come,' I assured him, trying to alleviate his fears. Deep down, I had the urge to remind my brother that facing a tough situation required more than stones and bottles, it demands mental strength and resilience. However, I held back, realising that now was not the time for such a discussion. I left it for another day, hoping that things would calm down soon.

But our sleep had evaporated amid the hubbub and my nerves were on edge. I desperately needed something to calm myself. I requested my father for some brandy, for I knew he kept a good-quality bottle in his cupboard. Soon, he handed me a glass, and I downed the contents in one quick gulp.

With a newfound sense of calm, relaxed and perhaps a little tipsy, I returned to bed. My wife and our younger son lay awake, anticipating my return. As I lay down, I found comfort in singing an old song, finding refuge in its familiar melody.

चिंगारी कोई भड़के, तो सावन उसे बुझाये
सावन जो अगन लगाए, उसे कौन बुझाए?

(The monsoon rain extinguishes a spark
But what if the monsoon breeze starts a fire?)

As I repeated these lines, my younger son chimed in, lisping, 'Papa, *ichhme dalne ki kya baat hai, fial bligade bula lenge.*' (Papa, what is there to worry about? We will call the fire brigade.) My wife and I laughed, embracing our child's innocent wisdom and cherishing the purity of his words. In that moment, I pondered on what it would be like if the adult world could retain a child's simplicity.

Epilogue

In November 2019, the Supreme Court of India ruled that the site where the Babri Masjid had once stood should be handed over to a trust to build a Hindu temple, and a mosque constructed on an alternate site.

A consecration ceremony of the Ram Temple in Ayodhya was held on January 22, 2024, presided over by Prime Minister Narendra Modi. Uttar Pradesh Chief Minister Yogi Adityanath and Rashtriya Swayamsevak Sangh chief Mohan Bhagwat also attended and participated in the ceremony. More than 7,000 guests from India and overseas were invited to the event, which was held during the Abhijit muhurat, considered auspicious for such a ritual.

Prime Minister Modi declared January 22 as the beginning of an era, signifying a cultural and spiritual awakening for lakhs of people. He proclaimed the construction of the Ram Temple not just as a Hindi religious landmark but also as a representation of

India's diverse heritage and the victory of faith and perseverance.

~

Decades before these developments, during those four arduous days in 1992 right after the mosque had been demolished, I recall having a vivid dream. It was the night I returned home after four days and nights at the City Telephone Exchange. I had drifted effortlessly into sleep, and I dreamt I was behind the wheel of my blue Mahindra Jeep. Its engine hummed steadily as I rode down a winding road. The cassette player in the jeep whirred into life at my command, and a melodious song filled the car, repeating the words I had heard in the dream with Aziz and his three victims: '*Ek aisa raja ayega jo gurbat say hamhey uthayega, jo mandir bhi banwayega aur Ram Rajya bhi layega.*'

In this dream, the same words held a much deeper meaning for me. They heralded the arrival of a benevolent ruler who would build temples, uplift the downtrodden, and establish a kingdom of righteousness, reminiscent of the rule of Lord Rama.

Acknowledgements

This book is a meeting point for my passion—the technology that shaped the nation's communications facilities—and a story I felt compelled to tell. I hope readers will relate to both aspects of the narrative they are about to read.

DK Gupta and Gokul Singh, my bosses in Bhopal, thank you for inspiring me to care about the people we officers are put in charge of.

All officers and employees, members of unions and associations, and others I worked with throughout my career: I hope you find this story is as much about you as the characters in the novel.

I am immensely grateful to my parents, and to Tripti, my wife, and my children, Mohit and Ankit. I could not have done it without your inspiration and support.

I would like to extend my sincere gratitude to all the customers of BSNL who may have cancelled their telephone subscriptions due to 'Bhai Sahab Nahi

Lagta'. I hope you will understand our side of it one day. Someday, I promise, the real reason for 'Bhai Sahab Nahi Lagta' will be revealed.

My special thanks go to all those writers-in-retirement who warned me not to write a 'technical' book on telecommunications.

Thanks to the editors at Speaking Tiger Books for making this more manageable.

And last but not least, Mihir Shrivastava, thank you for believing this book could be a book.